LONGSIGHT M40

TYLER JONES

LETHE
PRESS

Longsight M40
© 2025 by Tyler Jones

ISBN 9781590218112

For more information about Lethe Press publications, visit us at: lethepressbooks.com

Cover and interior art by Ben Baldwin

Cover and interior design by Scott Cole | 13visions.com

For more information about the author, visit tylerjones.net

To Phil Haagensen

For friendship and insight

BY TYLER JONES

Longsight M40

Night of the Long Knives

Turn Up the Sun

Heavy Oceans

Midas

Burn the Plans

Enter Softly

Almost Ruth

The Dark Side of the Room

Criterium

SOUTHBOUND ON I-5

A CONVOY OF SEMI-TRUCKS and buses rumbles south down the interstate in the early morning hours. The sky is overcast, filled with gray clouds, and fog rolls across the mountains as the city of Portland recedes in the distance. A graveyard scene has been painted on the trailer at the front of the caravan. A rogue's gallery of ghouls and monsters, rendered in a bright and bloody comic book style. The words **FRIGHT FAIR** are emblazoned across the metal with a website address beneath them.

Five semi-trucks carry an assortment of Halloween decorations, animatronics, fog machines, costumes, paint, fake blood, fake severed limbs and heads. There are decals, rubber bats and snakes, tentacles, prop knives, sledgehammers, and chainsaws. Realistic looking eyeballs and intestines, and all the parts required to construct a mad scientist's laboratory, including towers made of coils that shoot bright electric currents.

The buses are a second home for the employees of the Fright Fair—a collection of lost individuals who do not want to be found, their meager possessions jammed into backpacks and duffel bags. Theirs is a vampiric lifestyle of sleeping during the day and working at night. Some of the employees will vanish in one town, never to be seen or heard from again. Others will return each season, looking a little more weathered, a little more hardened. There is a code, a language, a hierarchy to the crew. If the employees have one thing in common, it's that they are all looking for something more than what they have.

Liquor bottles are opened and passed around. A poker game is played on a suitcase being used as a makeshift table. The cabin is filled with cigarette and weed smoke. It is soaked into the upholstery and creates a thin yellow film on the windows. A few people are in love, and they spoon under a blanket in the back. Some hate each other and the tension as they pass in the narrow aisle is felt by all.

Every four days the crew drives to a new destination and transform the town's fairgrounds into a spectacle of horror and fun.

Any passing motorist with a morbid curiosity about the convoy would find the following on the Fright Fair website:

**WHY SHOULDN'T HALLOWEEN LAST EVEN LONGER?
WHY SHOULDN'T WE CARRY THE FUN, THE SCARES,
THE CHILLS AND THRILLS INTO NOVEMBER AND BEYOND?
COME CELEBRATE ALL THINGS MACABRE AND SPOOKY
WITH US AT THE FRIGHT FAIR, A UNIQUE HALLOWEEN
THEMED FAIR TRAVELING THE COUNTRY WITH
FOUR DAY STOPS IN A TOWN NEAR YOU!**

Harvey Jessup sits alone on the bus with a gas station cup of coffee warming his hands. He stares out the window as the scenery flies by. The bus is filled with the coughs, sneezes, hiccups, and yawns of dozens of other employees, each of them still waking up, though Harvey knows some of them never went to sleep. No matter what town they're in, Byron has some sketchy friend who can score cocaine, or meth, or another substance that'll make your skeleton vibrate like a tuning fork and keep your eyes open wide for days on end.

Harvey hates that shit now, but he didn't always.

He towers over most of the other hundred or so employees who travel together, set up, and run the Fright Fair. At 6'7" he's an imposing figure. Completely bald, bearded, with an impressive collection of tattoos decorating his arms and creeping up his neck, at least half of them acquired in prison.

Most everyone is afraid of him, but Harvey can't help that. He doesn't think of himself as a violent person, even though he has the capacity for violence. But who doesn't? He tried to give his anger a healthy outlet in semi-professional boxing for a while, but he got his bell rung one too many times and it started to affect his mood.

Because of his size and physique, in his old life, Harvey rarely had to fight. Most of the time, just him showing up and standing there was enough to make people think twice before crossing him. But if things ever went sideways, he was able to flip a switch in his brain and become a human wrecking ball. A force of destruction. An artist painting walls with blood and teeth. A skill that was useful during his time as an enforcer for The Phantoms—a motorcycle club that ran drugs and dealt in prostitution and gambling on the side—also gave him the family he never had growing up. Harvey was brought in to assist during shakedowns, and he was good at it. He has a gentle way of speaking that can be both comforting and threatening, depending on the situation.

Harvey always knew riding with The Phantoms could end him up in prison, but in a twist of fate, it was a bar fight over a five-dollar bet on a pool game that got him locked up. The guy he was playing lost and refused to pay, so Harvey cracked him over the head with a pool cue and put the gouger in a coma with a brain bleed.

Four years later, Harvey walked out of Chino Men's Prison determined to avoid chaos and trouble. He had enough of that to last a lifetime. When he saw an ad for the Fright Fair, he decided to apply, not realizing it would involve extensive travel. Harvey didn't care. A job is a job, and he needed money and a place to stay, something the Fair provided.

He has been free for exactly eight weeks and working for the Fair for five of those. He keeps to himself and doesn't talk to anyone. Occasionally, someone will try and crack his hard exterior, to "get his story." But Harvey only nods and smiles politely and goes back to his work. It's simple work, manual labor, and Harvey finds it meditative. He is able to lift and move heavy objects for hours on end, so he sees it as getting paid to work out.

He has been trained as a maintenance man, so after the Fair is set up, he wanders from ride to ride, from booth to booth, fixing anything that needs fixed—replacing decals, lightbulbs, greasing tracks, repairing fog machines. It affords Harvey plenty of time to think about what he wants out of life. He isn't certain yet, but he catches a glimpse of it sometimes. A distant and blurry image that gets a little clearer each day.

Today, however, his head is as foggy as the landscape. He didn't sleep well last night. Dreams again. Nightmares in which he is enraged with someone and cannot stop himself from unleashing his fury. Harvey woke up from these dreams drenched in sweat and shaking. They felt so real he turned on a light and inspected his knuckles for blood.

The capacity for violence is still inside him, and his brain doesn't want him to forget.

He sits alone, swaying with the motion of the bus, ignoring the commotion all around him.

Today, the Fair is driving to Medford, Oregon, where they will transform and operate the Jackson County Fairgrounds. Four nights in town, then they will pack up and move on to the next. Harvey is in charge of unloading truck number two when they arrive. At least a quarter of the trailer is shit they never use. Things that break down and fall apart are loaded up again and carted to the next town, and if things are slow, Harvey will try and repair those items before they pack up again.

Inside that trailer is an object Harvey despises and fears with his whole being. A heavy rectangular box kept under a canvas tarp. He can picture the object at that moment, swaying back and forth, testing the limits of the straps that hold it in place.

Of all the rooms he's been in, with people who have done some of the most horrific things he'd ever heard of, it's that box that makes him the most nervous he's ever been.

Whenever he's near it, sweat droplets immediately appear, like magic, all over his face and back. He's thought of abandoning the box in one of these shithole towns and lying to his boss, saying he simply forgot to load it. But it looks expensive, and he doesn't want to lie. Not anymore. He wants to be better. Near the end of his stint in prison, Harvey thought he had his temper under control. But goddamn if he didn't start dreaming violence the night after he first touched that box.

1

EVEN THOUGH IT'S AN OLD, ugly beater with a whiny engine and an exhaust pipe that spews a toxic cloud every time Clay turns the key, that 2004 Toyota Corolla—with a quarter of a million miles on the odometer, toothpaste blue—is an escape.

For the last year, Mom and Dad have been fighting worse than ever. Before the car, Clay would hide in his room and put on headphones to drown out the sound of their screaming voices. But even then, he knew what was happening in the other room. He could feel the vibration of Dad's foot as it slammed down on the floor to emphasize his accusations. The walls and floors shivered with violence whenever something was slammed, thrown, kicked, or punched.

Scars on the furniture, gouges in the walls. Sometimes, Clay would find fragments of a ceramic coffee mug between the couch cushions days after an argument.

Even though Dad never hit Mom, and as far as Clay knew, she never hit him, the words were violent enough. They tore each other to pieces. All the worst things a person could say, they screamed at each other. Clay once thought he'd like to be married someday, but as time went on and the fighting dragged out in an endless war with no victor, he started thinking about how crazy it is for two people to commit to spending the rest of their lives together when they're still so young.

You grow to hate what's always right in front of you.

Clay spent most of the summer saving money for his first car. He collected cans and turned them in at the grocery store for cash. He rode his bike around the neighborhood and offered to do odd jobs like cleaning gutters, mowing lawns, walking dogs. Anything and everything that put a little extra money toward his escape.

Dad told him not to get the Corolla, told him to save more for a better vehicle, but Clay couldn't wait any longer. He hated the fighting.

In school, he read about how Mount Vesuvius exploded and destroyed the ancient city of Pompeii, and he imagines he knows exactly how those people felt as fire rained down from the sky, and a dark cloud of ash and smoke blotted out the sun.

Clay lives under the same shadow, and it's only a matter of time before the seismometer goes crazy. And even though he hates the idea of his parents getting divorced, as a sophomore in high school, splitting his time between houses is better than living through the earthquakes and tremors of their marriage. If all goes according to plan, Clay will move out in just a few short years anyway. Maybe college, maybe trade school. He hasn't decided yet. A divorce would seem so much worse if he were younger.

He knows it's inevitable. One of these days, he'll come home from school and the house will be quiet. Mom and Dad will have him sit on the couch and they'll both be calm—that'll be the sign it's happening—and they'll explain how people grow apart over time. It's not Clay's fault—even though he's heard his name spit out a few times as the reason for one fight or another—and they both still love him very much, but they will be separating. Clay's life will be ripped in half—a bedroom at Mom's house, and a bedroom wherever Dad moves. Probably a shitty apartment somewhere, because he'll have to pay alimony and child support, and you can't really afford much after all that money is gone.

Clay is the only one in his friend group with a car, and even though it's a turd on wheels, it's still a car that can take him, Kenny, Joel, and Harper anywhere they want to go. Yeah, his friends' parents aren't thrilled that a sixteen-year-old who just got his license is driving their kids around, but Medford isn't a big town, and cops are everywhere on account of all the meth-heads and fentanyl pushers. It's safer than walking, anyway.

It's a Friday in early November, and Clay wakes up to a mist-shrouded morning and the smell of fresh coffee. He's just started drinking the stuff, not because he likes it, but because he had to get up so early all summer to earn money for the car. Now, he's used to it, and in a small way, the cup of dark liquid makes him feel more grown up.

Like being adult means swallowing shit you don't like. Times infinity until you die.

Dad is already off to work by the time Clay showers and makes his way into the kitchen. Mom sits at the little table, both hands gripping a steaming mug, wrapped in her bathrobe, her hair pulled into a messy ponytail. She stares out the window with watery eyes, surrounded by red skin. She's lost weight. Not a lot, but enough for Clay to notice.

He doesn't know what to say, so he opens and closes the refrigerator louder than he needs to when he grabs the coffee creamer, just to let Mom know he's in the room.

She shivers a little, blinks a few times, and turns in her seat. She smiles when she sees her son. A series of small muscle movements that curl her lips and crease her cheeks, but she can't see how she looks. How fake that smile is.

"Morning, honey," she says. "Did you sleep alright?"

Clay takes a mug out of the cabinet and pours coffee over the creamer.

"Not bad. Some cats fighting woke me up once, but I fell back to sleep."

Mom makes a humming noise to acknowledge what he said.

"I packed your lunch," she says. "It's in the fridge."

She hasn't packed his lunch once this year. Ever since he started working odd jobs during the summer, he's taken on the responsibility himself. And, he became health-conscious not long after school started, which might have something to do with Harper. They've been friends since first grade, and that's all Clay ever saw her as—until this year..

Harper, the girl, disappeared somewhere back in June, at the beginning of summer. Harper, the woman, came rolling into sophomore year with makeup, a new wardrobe, and a maturity that set Clay's heart racing in a way he is still confused by. She told him she had taken up running during the summer, and her legs were lean and muscled, like a soccer player's, even though she didn't play soccer.

They texted a bit, but Clay hardly saw her during the summer since she went on several lengthy trips with her family and spent a month as a counselor at a camp for disabled children somewhere out in eastern Oregon. So, that first day back at school, Clay was not prepared for how much she'd changed. He wondered if she noticed anything different about him, or if he still looked the same.

"I made you a turkey and cheese sandwich," Mom says. "I hope that's okay."

Clay takes his lunch bag out of the fridge and opens it. There's the sandwich, along with a bag of pretzels and an apple. He feels a little childish with his Mom-packed lunch, but he thanks her and says it's perfect. This makes Mom smile, and maybe it's a little more real this time. Like, at least one man in her life is grateful for all she does.

Clay doesn't want to feel this way, doesn't want to carry that heavy awareness of another person's emotional life. On the other hand, he also feels something internal get stronger when he does.

Like, maybe this is also part of being an adult. Loving someone so much that their pain becomes yours, and this is how you help make it hurt less.

The way Mom sits with that cup in her hands, Clay has a blink-flash of her twenty years from now— older, more wrinkled, hair grayer, eyes cloudier. Her whole body leans toward him slightly, like she wants to be closer to her son but isn't sure how. Not anymore. Not this adolescent version of the boy she carried inside her, fed, clothed, taught, raised, loved, and disciplined. This new version is out of reach and she's not sure how to mother him. Not sure what use all those skills she acquired and honed over the years have now that he's sixteen and driving. Driving!

Clay senses her need in a deep place, and it makes him ache for her. He also knows, if he's honest with himself, that all the recent fighting has completely fucked up his allegiances. He doesn't know who to side with— Mom or Dad. Who's to blame? Who's in the wrong? When he was a kid, he used to pick sides and hope that parent won. These days, he thinks they're both wrong and the only way he knows how to react is to pull away from them both.

Mom feels it. Of course she does.

Clay sets his coffee mug on the counter and approaches Mom. She sits up straighter, eyes open wider. He leans and wraps his arms around her shoulders. She rests her head against his chest. He doesn't have words, but as he feels Mom's body shaking with silent tears, he realizes he doesn't need words.

2

AT SOME POINT IN THE last couple of weeks, Clay has learned he is subconsciously on the lookout for Harper between every class. He checks his hair in the bathroom more than he ever did. He tries to walk down the wall with not poise exactly, but a looseness, like he's more confident than he actually is.

Ever since Mom and Dad started fighting, really fighting, Clay has felt like the floor dissolved from the plane he was soaring in, leaving him free-falling through miles of empty sky. He's felt disconnected, afraid.

More than anything, he hopes none of the struggle shows on his face as he fights the current of students to get to his locker. He unlocks and opens the door, stacks his math and English books inside, grabs his history book, and is about to shut the door when a metallic *bang* explodes right next to his head.

The history book falls to the floor when Clay jumps backward, his ears ringing, his heart hammering, and he sees Kenny doubled over, laughing.

Even though Kenny is a couple of inches taller and more muscular, Clay resists the sudden urge to snatch a handful of his friend's hair and bash his face into the lockers.

"Dude, I swear," Clay says, "if you do that one more time—"

Kenny ignores him and crouches, staring intently at Clay's crotch.

Clay frowns and picks up his fallen book. "What the hell are you doing?"

"Just checking for piss stains," Kenny says, and laughs again.

Clay glances down on instinct, face reddening as he searches the crowd of students hustling from one class to another, hoping, for once, that Harper isn't nearby. Once he's certain she isn't around, Clay can't help but laugh, too. With his blonde hair and easy smile, it's hard not to get caught up in Kenny's mood, whatever it is. He's charismatic and careless. A reaction, Clay knows, to the storms Kenny faces at home.

Just last Friday, Clay drove over to Kenny's house and found him sitting on the sidewalk smoking a cigarette stolen from his dad, cheek red and puffy from the man's fist. His eyes were distant and watery, but as soon as they drove away, Kenny started testing out new material for his future comedy act. Four years ago, Kenny's mom decided she cared more about getting high than she did her husband and son. And ever since, there's been no one to stand between Kenny and his dad's temper.

"Friday night, man," Kenny says. "You got the wheels, you make the plan. What are we doing?"

"I don't know," Clay says. "Go to a movie?"

"Nah, we went to a movie last week. And there's nothing good. I checked."

"Miniature golf?"

Kenny shakes his head. "Too many little kids farting around that place. Anything happening at the Orchard?"

One of Medford's primary exports is pears, and through years of tradition, the largest pear orchard is a place where high schoolers go to drink, get high, and even fight. In Medford, it's not "See you out back," it's, "See you at the Orchard." A time is set, a circle is formed, and the two contenders go at it until one of them is bloody and unconscious, while the crowd cheers on the spectacle.

"Not that I know of," Clay says.

They join a throng of students, shoulder to shoulder, more than half of them distracted by phones. One guy pushes another guy across the hall. He crashes through a group of girls on his way to the far wall.

A girl screams, "Fucking asshole," while her dropped phone is still in midair.

Clay's feet dance to avoid all the commotion. Kenny walks straight through, his strong arms brushing kids aside to make a path. Clay follows his friend's black puffy jacket and sneakers so teeth-commercial white they're easy to follow in the crowd.

Even though Kenny is Clay's closest friend, he couldn't explain—if pressed—why they're friends. It was never a choice, not really. More like gravity. Two kids born on the south side of town, where the houses sag with disrepair, children's toys lie scattered across unkempt lawns, and more cars sit idle than run. Broken glass glints like diamonds in the gutters. Dealers stroll the blocks with the casual swagger of regulars, nodding to passersby, waiting for someone to nod back. Sirens echo in the night. Sometimes gunshots too. The cars are rusted. The kids wear hand-me-downs or thrift shop finds. Their shoes don't fit, and the soles are splitting. There may not be money to patch the roof, but there's always money for cigarettes, beer, and lottery tickets. The families are blue-collar and worn thin, and the problems behind closed doors are ones everyone knows by heart.

The north side is another world.

A few minutes later, they make it to the stairs. Kenny stops halfway down with a snap of his fingers and turns, smiling.

"The Fright Fair starts tonight."

"Fright Fair?"

"Yeah," Kenny says and resumes his descent. "You know, rides, cotton candy, games?"

"I've been to the fair a thousand times. It's not that great."

"This one's different."

"Isn't it just the fair with Halloween decorations?"

"Yeah," Kenny says, with a straight face. "And that's what makes it great."

Clay thinks of his bank account, how he can barely afford to fill up his gas tank. "I'm low on funds, man," he says.

"We don't have to do anything," Kenny says, gently shoulder-checking a freshman in his way. The kid goes bumping into a stoner gazing up at the ceiling with a goofy grin. "It'll just be cool to hang out there. What else we gonna do?"

The real question is: what else is there to do?

They've done it all, a million times. They're too old for the arcade or the Fun Center, too young to drink at a bar or go to the dance club. Too old for the ice cream shop, too young to buy booze. Sixteen, Clay thinks, is Limbo.

At the bottom of the stairs, Clay says, "All right, let's check out the fair," but Kenny ignores him. He has his phone in hand, screen tilted at an awkward angle so Clay can't see it. He types something with one thumb, not even watching where he's going.

"I said, let's do it. Let's go to the fair."

"Yeah, I heard you," Kenny says, as they enter Mr. Pine's classroom. Maps of famous battlefields hang on the walls, black and white photos of young soldiers, mud-splattered and screaming, rushing headfirst into violence. Photos of an atomic explosion, the decimation of Hiroshima and Nagasaki.

Mr. Pine sits behind his desk, taking sips from a coffee mug while looking over his glasses as students file in. It might not be filled with actual coffee. Occasionally, he points silently at the phone holder on the wall—a three-by-three-foot square with over two dozen pockets for cell phones—and keeps pointing until each student has slipped their phone into one of the slots.

The boys find Joel in the back row, reading a book with wizards and elves on the front cover. He nods without looking up at them, and turns a page in his book. The books he reads are the only nerdy thing about Joel. Mostly, he's obsessed with cars, with engines and speed and danger. At home, he and his dad are in the process of rebuilding the engine of a 1973 Ford Cortina they found rusting behind the barn at an estate sale. A project they've been working on for over a year.

Clay and Kenny sit on either side of Joel. Kenny gently kicks Joel's desk until he puts down the book and looks at his friend with an irritated expression. His dark curly hair falls in ringlets around his eyes. He wears a brown Carhartt jacket over a grey hoodie, and his jeans (every single pair he owns) have grease stains on them.

"Fright Fair tonight. You in?" Kenny asks.

Joel slides a worn bookmark in between the pages and closes the book. "I'm in," he says. "Can't stay out too late, though. Me and Dad are test driving the Cortina tomorrow."

"No way," Clay says. "It's finished?"

"Pretty much." Joel has this special smile he doesn't often share. "Still a few things we need to fix, but the engine is back together, and she runs. So now we just need to see if she drives."

Clay holds out a fist, and Joel bumps it with his own.

"Congrats, man," Clay says. "That's awesome."

Joel is the smartest person Clay knows. "An old soul," his mother once called him. He always seems to be thinking more deeply, dreaming bigger, and filling his mind with ideas. He possesses a maturity that no one else in the school has. An awareness of how big and important life is, or at least how it seems to Clay. Probably because his mom died when Joel was barely old enough to remember her. His dad never remarried.

Joel is the only person Clay has told about his new feelings for Harper, because Joel is the only person who would understand and not judge.

"What about Harper?" Joel asks. "Is she going?"

"Don't know yet…" Clay starts to say, but Kenny interjects.

"She's coming."

Clay gives him a confused look. "How do you know?"

"I texted her. She said she's in."

Kenny says this without looking at Clay, and it makes him feel something. Jealousy, maybe. He doesn't have time to analyze the feeling because Mr. Pine rises from behind the desk, and in a loud voice, tells the class to open their books to the chapter about the Battle of Stalingrad.

3

EVEN THOUGH CLAY LIVES JUST two blocks down the street from Kenny, he lies and says he has to get something for his mom on the other side of town, so he'll pick up Harper first, then Joel, and Kenny last. A small lie that gives him and Harper fifteen minutes alone in the car. He only saw her briefly at lunch, since they don't have any classes together, and he's wanted to talk to her all day. In fact, his brain has been on fire ever since school started back up. Blazing with imagined conversations.

Almost every single night, he lies awake staring up into the darkness of his room and fantasizing about telling her how much she means to him. How he thinks about her all the time.

Clay understands there is a right way and a wrong way to do this, to tell a person they mean so much to you that nearly every waking hour is interrupted with thoughts of them.

He doesn't want to say it like they do in movies, because every girl has probably heard those same words, said in that same order, way too many times. He wants to somehow find the exact right words to explain how *he* feels about *her*.

He whispers out loud to the ceiling, testing each word, each phrase. Sometimes they're cheesy but honest. Sometimes they're just cheesy.

As Clay drives across town to Harper's, he wonders if tonight is the night. Does he pull over somewhere, say, "Harper, there's something I want to tell you?" Does he tell her while he's driving?

On the way home from school, Clay stopped at a gas station and bought a new package of those tree-shaped air fresheners. Vanilla, because one time Harper said she liked the smell of his car. His stupid, ugly, piece of shit car. She likes how it smells.

Once he got home, Clay spent the next two hours clearing out the trash, vacuuming, and washing the car until the turd sparkled. She probably won't notice, but maybe she will.

Every time Clay pulls up in front of Harper's house, he's reminded that she lives in another world. The whole neighborhood is beautiful, two-story homes with clean, double-paned windows, and lush green yards. Plants and flowers grow in the bark that surrounds each house.

Gleaming, European vehicles are parked in each driveway. Light and warmth radiate from between elegant curtains.

Suddenly, all the effort he put into cleaning the Corolla doesn't seem good enough.

He checked his hair five times before leaving his house, but Clay pulled down the visor and checked again. The pimple that's been growing on his chin for the last two days is angry and red. He snuck into Mom's bathroom and patted a tiny bit of skin-colored foundation over the spot, but he still sees it. Maybe Harper won't notice in the dark.

Satisfied the zit doesn't look like a third eyeball on his chin, Clay grabs his phone to text Harper he's waiting outside, then stops. That would be the typical thing to do. The thing that requires minimal effort.

Instead, he jams the phone back in his jacket pocket—a black puffer similar to Kenny's, although Clay got his first and was annoyed that Kenny immediately copied him—gets out of the car and makes his way up to the porch. Two white rockers sit off to one side with a small table between them. He's never seen anyone use the chairs, and they seem more for decoration than anything. The smell of a home-cooked feast drifts in the air as he gets closer to the front door. The kind of meal you see families having in movies, everyone gathered around a dining room table, telling each other about their day.

He knocks three times and waits, shivering in the night air.

A few heartbeats later, the door opens, and Harper stands there, smiling.

"Hey, Clay!" she says, her voice musical. She leans out of view for a moment to snatch a coat off a peg near the door, then calls over her shoulder, "See you guys!"

There is a clear view straight into the dining room where Mason, Harper's younger brother, sits at the table, head resting on one hand, pushing food around on his plate. Harper's mom comes out of the kitchen, and her smile is a photocopy of her daughter's. Effortless and warm.

She gives a little wave. "Hello, Clay. Be sure to let us know how the fair is. We're thinking of taking Mason this weekend."

"I will," Clay says.

A tall man in a button-down shirt and suit pants comes padding out of the living room in his socks. He shakes Clay's hand, gives his daughter a kiss on the forehead, and says to Clay, "Drive safe out there."

Clay says, "Of course," then gestures to his car. "That thing can't go over thirty miles an hour, anyway."

Harper's dad laughs. "I'm okay with that."

He reaches over and grabs his wallet from a small table and opens it up. His thumb grazes over a thick stack of bills. With thumb and forefinger, he pulls out a ten and hands it to Clay.

"Gas money," he says. "It's not cheap these days."

Clay is about to protest, about to say he doesn't need it, when Harper says, "Thanks, Dad."

"Do you need any extra cash?"

Harper shakes her head. "I'm good."

"Here, take twenty, just in case."

Harper takes the money and goes on tiptoe to kiss her dad's cheek. "I'll call when we're on our way back," she says. "Love you guys!"

Both her mom and dad echo the sentiment as she closes the door behind them. Harper skips down the walkway, hands in her pockets, shoulders hunched.

"Woo! It's brutal."

"I'll crank the heat," Clay says, and has a moment of panic as Harper nears his car. Does he open the door for her? Has he ever done that? Will it seem too... formal, if he does?

Thankfully, Harper doesn't wait for him. She opens the passenger side door herself and gets in. When Clay slides behind the wheel, he turns the heat all the way up and pulls away from her house. The car that previously smelled of vanilla is now filled with Harper's perfume. A lovely floral scent he can't get enough of. It's a popular perfume amongst high school girls, but it smells different on her. Like it mixes with her skin and forms a magical chemical reaction.

Since Clay drove to her house lost in thought, he forgot to turn the radio on, and he wonders if he should do so now. But then he'd have to turn it back off if he parks somewhere so they can talk.

Harper's long coat is brownish-red plaid with a hood. It looks elegant and expensive. The kind of coat a woman would wear, not a girl. In fact, she looks so much older tonight. She usually wears a small amount of make-up, but as they come to a stop at a red light, Clay glances over and notices the eyeshadow, the mascara, and the lipstick. He notices the way her shoulder-length auburn hair is curled in the back and pinned up in the front with a single barrette.

She sits up straight, hands folded in her lap, a half-smile on her face as she talks about the fair and how she's going to eat so much cotton candy she'll be sick, because it's been forever since she's had it.

One of the things he likes about Harper is the way she defies any easy categorization. Every other girl in school fits into some mold with its own predetermined set of rules, clothes, attitude, and language. Athlete. Stoner. Brainiac. Skater. Slacker. Actress. Slut. Goth. Pick a movie about high school and you'll see each group represented in one of the characters. Some cliches exist because they're true, though. A high school is a building packed full of teenagers with hormones on overdrive, all trying to figure out who they are in the world.

Harper already seems to know, and Clay is drawn to this certainty.

He's sure she probably has insecurities, but none of them are evident. Other girls complain of depression, anxiety, and stress. Clay doesn't think Harper is above those emotions, she just somehow processes them differently. To the point that she seems to be the only solid object in a blurry world. A thing of clarity in a place of chaos.

It's exhilarating and terrifying to him.

She doesn't even listen to the music everyone else does. Her favorite band is The Cranberries, unironically. She has posters of Dolores O'Riordan on her walls.

Clay has seen her bedroom exactly once, and he felt like an astronaut on a distant planet, observing each detail of the space—the cluttered dresser with its array of knickknacks, the corkboard with photographs of family and friends, the vinyl records stored in an old blue milk crate, the books on the shelves, the pile of clothes spilling out of the closet, and the stuffed animals on the bed (a relic and reminder that not all that long ago she was still just a girl)—like he had to file a scientific report with the Society of Interstellar Species.

The shapes of all the words Clay wants to say are emblazoned on the forefront of his mind like a neon sign in the window of a bar. Words that will make her fall in love with him. Words that not only mean but actually express all that's in his heart.

His mouth goes dry as he imagines saying them. His lips and tongue test the words silently. His heart thuds so hard it's uncomfortable and makes him feel weak.

"You missed the turn," Harper says, looking at him with a smile that causes him to swallow so hard it burns his chest.

"What?"

"The turn," she says. "For Joel's house."

He lets out a small laugh that sounds like a hiccup and makes a left to head back to the road he'd missed. He didn't realize how close they were to Joel's. Clay desperately tries to think of a nearby place where he could park the car. Is he being awkward? He feels awkward.

"You okay?" she asks, her face a sudden and tender expression.

Clay's stomach clenches. His fingers tremble on the steering wheel. He opens his mouth again. He's going to say the words. He's going to say he has something important to tell her when Harper's phone buzzes.

Her face lights up in the glow of the screen as she checks the message, then laughs.

"It's Kenny. He wants to know what's taking us so long."

Clay shuts his mouth, gritting his teeth together. He pictures Kenny, sitting in his room waiting for Clay's shitty car to pull up to the curb, and somehow, *somehow*, he has this sixth sense telling him what Clay is about to do. So, he opens his phone and texts Harper to completely ruin the moment and shove Clay back down where he belongs.

Now, Clay grips the steering wheel with trembling fingers. The polyurethane creaks as his hands squeeze tighter, like they're wrapped around Kenny's neck.

Clay tries to smile and laugh along with Harper. "Tell him we decided to ditch him," he says, and laughs again when he realizes how unfunny the statement sounded in his tight voice. Harper smiles and begins texting Kenny back. Clay flips on the radio. A fucking song about lost love comes pouring out of the speakers.

4

JOEL COMES JOGGING OUT OF his house, curls bouncing under a knit beanie, breath streaming behind him. He gets in the backseat, says "Hey" to Harper, and passes a few wrinkled dollar bills to Clay for gas.

Harper and Joel chat as Clay navigates the streets that lead them to Kenny's house, back to Clay's own neighborhood. Harper is rarely in this area, but she knows where he lives and has been to his house several times over the years. Now, more than ever, though, Clay is painfully aware of how distant his neighborhood is from Harper's. Not just in terms of miles.

As they turn onto his street, Harper texts Kenny, and they find him already waiting at the curb, bundled in a puffy jacket, his nose red from the cold. He tumbles into the car, trailing an overpowering cloud of body spray— an attempt to cover the smell of cigarette smoke—and radiating the jittery energy of a kid who's sugar high and up way past his bedtime. He doesn't offer any money for gas, and Clay doesn't ask.

Clay feels like a babysitter when he asks if everyone has their seatbelts on, and Kenny says, "Yes, mother." Of course he does.

Joel starts to say something about how most accidents occur within two miles of home when Kenny punches Joel's leg hard enough to make him howl. Clay hits the accelerator, and the four friends glide through their dark town to the outskirts, where the Fright Fair is set up in an array of brightly lit rollercoasters and crisscrossing spotlights that scrape the sky.

5

IT'S KENNY'S IDEA TO SNEAK into the fair.

He doesn't say it's because he doesn't have the money, but that much is understood. Instead, he says they should do it because "it'll be fun." It seems that miles of chain-link fence have been set up to surround the perimeter of the fairgrounds, and there is only one entrance that can be seen from the parking lot.

"It's five bucks," Joel says. "That's not worth the risk."

"What risk?" Kenny says.

Joel starts counting on his fingers, "Oh, I don't know. Climbing the fence and falling over the other side. Getting caught by security and kicked out, probably arrested."

"They wouldn't arrest me."

"Or, best case scenario, you sit outside in the cold for hours while the rest of us have fun."

Kenny waves his hand, like brushing away a bad smell. "Whatever, man."

"Hypothermia, dehydration, death," Joel keeps counting.

"Fine, you guys go wait in line and I'll see you inside."

Kenny shoves his hands in his pockets and goes marching off toward the back fence. Clay is reminded, yet again, how fragile his friend's ego is. Has he always been like that? He thinks every idea that appears in his head is brilliant, and any challenge to its perfection makes him all moody and irritable.

Though Clay doesn't have the words for it, he instinctively understands that Kenny's desire to break things—whether it's rules or relationships—is directly connected to the brokenness he feels inside. It's part of why Clay can never bring himself to cut off the friendship, even when he wants to sometimes.

The three of them stand there, watching Kenny's silhouette get smaller and smaller, then Harper breaks away and jogs after him.

Clay wants to ask, but it's Joel who says, "What are you doing?"

Hair the color of blood in sunlight, Harper turns her head and shouts, "I'm hopping the fence!"

The boys watch in silence for a few moments, then Joel shrugs, and Clay says, "What the hell?" And they both trudge after their friends, weaving through the packed parking lot, through broad circles of diffuse light that illuminate tiny, sparkling drops of mist.

Hands in his pockets, shoulders hunched against the cold, Clay says, "I think I'm going to tell her tonight."

Joel looks down at his feet, sidestepping puddles. "Tell who what?"

"Harper. I think I'm going to tell her how I feel."

Joel scrunches up his face.

"What's that mean?" Clay says.

"What's what mean?"

Clay makes the same face Joel did. "That was you. Your face. You made a face."

Joel is the only one who knows. The only one Clay has confided in about his secret crush. But is crush even the right word? Is it just a crush if you think about someone for weeks, no, months on end? When those thoughts are more selfless than selfish, is that a crush or something more? Clay isn't sure, but it feels bigger. Deeper.

"It'll change the dynamic," Joel says, eyes wandering over all the cars. "But you know that already."

"Yeah, but we're not kids anymore. The dynamic, whatever it is, will change eventually anyway."

Joel nods and zips his coat all the way to his neck. "Have you thought about how it will go? What she'll say?"

"A million times," Clay says, trying not to smile. Even just talking about it gives his blood a carbonated feeling, like it's lifting out of his veins.

"Sure, but you've imagined it one way," Joel says. "Have you thought about if it doesn't go the way you want?"

The question almost freezes Clay in place. His feet stop moving and Joel passes three cars before pausing and turning around. Up ahead, Clay sees Kenny and Harper at a stretch of fence hidden in the dark, at the very back of the fairgrounds.

Joel backtracks until he's by Clay's side. "What I'm asking is, are you prepared to lose her as a friend?"

"You think it'll come to that?"

"If she doesn't feel the same way, it's up to you whether you can handle seeing her with another guy. If you can be happy for her and treat her the same as you always have. If not, yeah, it'll definitely come to that."

"Shit," Clay whispers.

"Yep," Joel agrees. "Shit."

Kenny's voice carries across the distance, "Gentlemen, sometime this year would be fantastic," followed by Harper's musical laugh.

Joel bumps his shoulder into Clay's. "Come on."

When they make it to the fence, Clay can't feel his nose or ears, and wishes he'd thought to bring a beanie, like Joel did.

Kenny, breath coming out in clouds as he speaks, points up at the tall chain-link fence. "I'll go over first to test it out. Then Harper, so I can help her down the other side."

They are far past all the attractions, out where the semi-trucks and trailers that transported the fair are stored. A collection of old tents, house crates, and tool chests, tubs of grease, and extra bulbs. The backstage of the Fright Fair.

Before Clay can think to protest, Kenny jumps and clings to the fence, fingers hooked into the metal diamonds, shoes scraping for a toehold. The entire fence sways with his weight. For a second, it looks like he might lose his grip and tumble back down to the asphalt, but he scrambles up higher until he's able to throw one leg over the top, twist his body over the jagged points, and climb down the other side.

He stands facing the other three and makes a dramatic bow, like he'd just scaled a mountain in the Himalayas. It takes all of Clay's self-control to not roll his eyes and try to make it over the fence even faster just to prove something to…who?

"Okay, me next," Harper says, smiling. Always smiling, as if being alive and experiencing anything, no matter how insignificant, is the height of existence. She unbuttons her coat so the flaps swing free. She grabs hold of the fence and starts to climb, but she struggles to get the tips of her boots into the small holes.

"Guys, give me a boost," she says.

Clay moves into position underneath and swallows hard. If this was Joel, or even Kenny, he'd push on his butt to help him, but he can't do that. Can he? Thankfully, Joel stands on the other side and puts his hands under one of Harper's feet, providing a stirrup. Clay mentally kicks himself, and does the same, glancing over at Joel's face so he doesn't give in to the temptation to stare at Harper's ass as she climbs upward. He wants to be a gentleman. He wants to be the kind of man *she* wants.

Harper's feet leave their hands a few moments later, and by the time Clay steps back, she's already over the top and halfway down the other side. One boot slips, knocking loose the other, and she dangles by her fingers.

"I can't hold on!" she yells.

It's not very high, but it scares her. Kenny holds out both hands and tells her to let go. Tells her he'll catch her. She looks over her shoulder, an expression of pain on her face, and releases her fingers. That beautiful coat catches the breeze, and it flutters open on either side of her body like plaid wings. Her eyes are closed. Kenny's strong hands are ready, and they grab her waist, slowly lowering her down until her feet touch the ground.

The sight of them so close—his hands touching her, the smile on her face—is enough to make Clay shrink inside. He understands there are small moments and brief interactions that can act as a revelation between people. Like a switch is flipped from friendship to romance, and his stomach is sick thinking he's witnessing one of those moments from the other side of a see-through barrier.

A shift in the dynamic, like Joel said. Only he isn't part of the change.

He grabs the fence and climbs as fast as he can, praying to God he doesn't fall or make a fool of himself. Twenty seconds later, he's standing next to Harper and Kenny, wondering if he can position himself between them. Joel scales the fence next, and when he jumps down with a grunt, Kenny says, "Alright, let's go," and takes off running. The other three friends can't help but smile and run after him, toward the lights and sounds and twisting fake bodies that dangle from each car of the Ferris Wheel that spins across the sky in slow revolutions.

6

AS FAR AS CLAY CAN tell, the Fright Fair is just a regular fair with more Halloween decorations. Every ride is a monster, every booth a portal to a dark dimension. All the workers are dressed in torn suits and dresses, their faces covered in green makeup and fake, oozing sores. They lumber around, grunting and growling at the children.

It all has a cheesy, low-production-value atmosphere and special effects that are almost endearing in the dark. Blacklights illuminate dripping handprints at the entrance to a rollercoaster called The Void. Each car has a purple spiral that suggests hypnosis. The tower drop ride is a snake-eyed monster at the top, and the four seats surrounding the tower crank slowly up toward its venom-soaked fangs, only to send you plummeting away from the creature's gaping mouth.

The baseballs for the bottle toss are decorated like eyeballs with red veins.

There are a few additions that are not part of a normal county fair, though. Like the Tarot card booth, the mind reader, the sword swallower, and the flame eater. Yes, the fair is kind of old-fashioned, and the small rollercoasters barely get your heart pumping unless you are ten years old. Even at sixteen, Clay still kind of loves how the fair lights up the night sky. No matter where you are in town, you can always see it. Always find it. Those bright multicolored lights ripple along the underbelly of dark clouds. If you turn the radio off and listen, you can hear the faint music of the calliope as gentle as birdsong. There's a charm to it all: the games and prize booths, the scent of cotton candy and churros, the men in dime-store Halloween costumes calling out to kids with voices like auctioneers.

Everything is bright and mechanical. Everything spins and dazzles and disorients. A man dressed as a vampire waves you over to a table where he has set up a game of three-card monte. The table next to him is operated by a man with a prominent brow and large bolts glued to either side of his neck, sliding around three red cups and a white ping pong ball. The two men have a well-rehearsed banter that gets the crowd laughing, drawing closer, reaching for wallets.

Somewhere there's a magician weaving through the crowd, his burgundy top hat emblazoned with golden spirals. He pulls a quarter from behind the ear of a child whose mouth first gapes in surprise, then squeals with delight. The magician reaches into a woman's purse and whips out an entire bouquet of flowers, which he then presents to the woman's husband so he can gift the arrangement to his wife.

A sense of joy and wonder trails behind the magician like the train of a bride's wedding dress.

A summer fair is all primary colors and smiles. This Fright Fair is full of blacks, greens, purples, and reds. Fake blood, painted blood, runs down every surface. Eyeballs blink, spiders leap, and monsters lurk everywhere you look.

Harper decides she wants to ride the Terror Wheel—which is just the Ferris Wheel with blood dripping down the sides of the cars and mannequin corpses hanging from the spokes—so she and Kenny race ahead to get in line. Clay doesn't want to go on the ride, but he can't let Kenny be alone with Harper, so he follows along and waits in line behind them.

They talk and Harper laughs easily, occasionally touching Kenny's chest with a brush of her hand when he says something especially amusing. Clay can't hear any of what they're saying. There's noise all around him, noise inside him.

He stares at Kenny and compares himself. He can't help it.

What does he have that Clay doesn't, other than the fact that they are very different people in every way?

Clay wishes Kenny didn't come, that he were somewhere else. A thought explodes into Clay's mind, a desire accompanied by a visual so crisp and clear it shocks him, then makes him ashamed. He imagines a few hours into the past, getting a text from Kenny saying he can't go tonight. Saying his dad gave him two nasty black eyes and he can barely see through the swollen slits of his eyelids.

The force with which Clay wishes this had happened is almost frightening. He turns to Joel, wide-eyed, as if his friend might have somehow heard the thought—or glimpsed the secret desire flickering behind it. But Joel just stares up at the Terror Wheel, at all those fake bodies, some with missing limbs and torn open chests, swinging from the ride like grotesque Christmas decorations.

When it's their turn to climb aboard, Clay tries to shoulder his way to the front so he can sit with Harper and Kenny, but the zombie ride attendant holds out an arm to stop him.

"Hold your horses, kid," he growls. "Only two per car."

Clay steps back, not even surprised to find his right hand clenched into a fist. Kenny doesn't seem to notice the commotion as he and Harper go up the stairs and climb into the waiting car. A moment later, the wheel turns, bringing another car to the platform. Two kids exit, and the zombie attendant waves Clay and Joel up. The boys take their seats, and the car jerks into motion, making Clay's stomach lurch.

Clay has a perfect view of Harper and Kenny in profile. Talking, laughing.

Once all the cars are full, the wheel begins its lazy spin. The air grows colder the higher they climb, and during the first curve, Harper and Kenny's car slides above him, out of view.

"Sorry it didn't go like you hoped," Joel says.

Clay looks down at the fair, at all the lights, and the crowds made up of small people moving from one attraction to another. Beyond that is the town of Medford, a series of orange and yellow lights glowing in silver mist.

He doesn't know what to say. He feels something like motion sickness, but it has nothing to do with the ride.

"It's not his fault," Joel says.

Clay nods, knows this is true, but he can't convince himself to believe it, even though Kenny had no idea how Clay felt. Maybe if he'd said something, Kenny would've acted differently. Still, Clay thinks, a thief is a thief, even if he didn't know he was robbing the house of a friend.

Soon, Joel and Clay's car is at the peak of the revolution, nothing but sky above them. Clay looks up at the clouds, and they seem close enough to touch. Harper and Kenny are now out of view, and he feels antsy with the sudden, irrational fear the wheel will break down, leaving them suspended in the sky, in the cold.

He turns slowly like he needs to scratch his shoulder, and Joel says, "Don't look, okay?"

"What? Why?"

"Just trust me, man. Don't look."

Clay twists his body until he sees the car behind them, sees Kenny with his lips on Harper's, one arm wrapped around her body, pulling her close. Clay closes his eyes, takes a deep breath, and opens them again. They're still kissing. Really kissing. Not just a gentle smooch, but tongues and jaws working.

All summer, Clay has fantasized, wondering what she tastes like. And now Kenny knows. For a moment, Clay imagines challenging Kenny to a fight at the Orchard to settle things. He pictures the circle of headlights, the jeers and shouts, the cold, hard dirt. He sees the twisted branches of the pear trees, tangled and leafless, looking like scarecrows in the moonlight. A secret crowd brought to life by the promise of teenage bloodshed on the packed, frozen earth.

But Clay knew he could never take Kenny. He was too hard and too angry.

An electrical surge shoots through Clay's body, shocking every nerve and bringing him back to the Terror Wheel. His hands grasp the safety bar and squeeze the frozen metal until he feels cold in his bones.

7

BY THE TIME THEIR CAR reaches the bottom, Harper and Kenny are already waiting for them not far from the line. Clay marches past the zombie attendant, down the rickety wooden stairs, and brushes right past Kenny without looking at him. Without saying a word.

He hears Harper say, "Is he all right?" and Joel responds, "Got nauseous up there."

Clay needs to stay in motion, to keep walking as fast and as far as he can, like his emotions are something that can be outrun. His hands clench into fists again and again. The anger, the betrayal he feels doesn't even make sense. But God how he feels it. And maybe it's worse that it's senseless, because in reality, it's his own failure that put him in this position.

Waiting, forever waiting for the "right moment" to tell Harper what he carries in his heart, as if there was a perfect bubble of time and opportunity he knew was somewhere in the future. A moment when every chaotic element of life would align for just a few seconds, and he could say what he needed to say. But he waited too long because that moment, that perfect bubble, never existed. They just happen, randomly, and Kenny was there when it appeared.

"Clay, wait up," Joel yells from behind him.

Clay wants to stop, to spill his guts to his friend, but he can't. He needs to keep moving, otherwise his chest might cave in.

He is surrounded by people—families, teenagers, kids—and they're all a blur. The lights are smears, the sounds of rides and games all distorted. He has no idea where he's going, only that his legs burn with the need to take him somewhere quiet.

Soon, the crowd thins out as he makes his way back toward the fence they'd climbed not long ago. Toward all the semi-trucks and trailers and tents that store odds and ends. Clay hears his own footsteps, and another set echoing behind him.

Clay stops, out of breath, and Joel catches up.

"Hey," he says. "You okay?"

Clay doesn't want his friend to see him cry, and if he says anything the tears will come, so he just nods, even though he is not okay. Not at all.

Joel nods too, hands on his knees, catching his breath.

"You walk fast, dude," he says with a smile.

"I can't be around them," Clay says. "I don't…I don't trust myself right now. Like I'll say something bad and ruin everything."

"Well, let's just stay here until it's time to go," Joel says.

"You sure?"

Joel stands up straight, mimes lighting an invisible cigarette between his lips, then all cool like, lowers it, makes a tiny O with his mouth, and blows out a cloud of vapor.

"Yeah. All the cool kids ditch their friends and hang out in the dark."

Clay can't help but smile. He turns his face to the sky and feels tiny drops land gently on his skin. He holds out a hand, palm up, and feels them there too.

"It's starting to rain."

Joel points two fingers, still holding that non-existent cigarette, toward the nearest tent.

"We can stay under there," he says. "They'll come back this way eventually."

Clay glances around quickly to see if there are any security guards, or employees wandering around, then jogs for the tent just as the tiny droplets grow in size. By the time they get under cover, heavy rain is pelting the roof of the tent. He and Joel turn in a circle, observing the haphazard stacks of equipment and tools, ropes, fasteners, and broken machines.

All the pieces of a Wild West shooting gallery are stacked in one corner, complete with tin bandits. The mallet from a "test your strength" game lies overturned nearby, one end cracked and broken. Squirt guns, a bucket full of bent darts, and torn decals of ghouls and goblins used to decorate various rides. A pirate's chest with a snapped lid, full of transparent plastic jewelry.

There are also large hydraulics, chains, and even a busted door from one of the Terror Wheel cars.

Clay walks slowly, observing each item, until he comes to the far corner where he notices a rectangular object, taller than he is, covered in an army-green canvas tarp, tucked behind what appears to be the dilapidated windmill from a miniature golf course.

This object stands out because it is the only one covered.

"Hey Joel," Clays says, pointing. "What do you think that is?"

Rain beats the tent, a sound like hundreds of squirrels frantically running across the fabric.

Joel squints into the dark. "Don't know. We got time, let's take a look."

Together, they lift and move the windmill, with its purposefully tattered wheel and crumbling stone, off to the side. Clay squats and pulls up a corner of the canvas tarp.

"No way," he whispers.

"What is it?"

Clay smiles, says nothing, and yanks the tarp off the object in one motion, exposing a tall wooden box that contains a human torso enclosed in glass.

8

JOEL TAKES IN A SHARP rush of breath. Hands no longer miming holding a cigarette but balled into fists.

Clay bursts out laughing at his friend's reaction.

Joel exhales, fingers unraveling. "What the hell?"

He steps closer and leans in, studying the face that stares back at him from behind the glass. An old man with wild white hair and leather, waxy skin. One arthritic hand—swollen knuckles and yellowed fingernails—hovers, clawlike, above a crystal ball. The other hand rests upon a deck of tarot cards, face up. The eyes are open so wide the boys can see the full circle of the pale blue irises. He wears a brown waistcoat and burgundy tie.

"It's a fortune-telling machine," Clay says, running his fingers along the wood to the metal slot where a ticket would appear. "Put in a coin, get a ticket with your fortune."

Only, there isn't a coin slot. Not that he can see, anyway. But there is a small metal handle, like a joystick, next to a small speaker that's flush with the wood.

"Dude does not look like a fortune teller," Joel says.

He's right. Every machine that Clay has seen depicts a man with a goatee wearing a turban, a bright jewel at its center, and a large hoop earring dangling from one ear. This one looks like a confused old man who got lost on his way back to the nursing home.

Painted in an elegant script across the upper edge of the glass are letters that spell out the word *Longsight*.

Also, the other machines Clay has seen at fairs and carnivals, even at the roller rink, were all made of hard plastic and metal. This entire box, except for the glass, is constructed from real wood that looks and feels old. Like the others, there is glass on the front and sides, giving him a view of the fortune teller from multiple angles.

Pushing aside a bucket of bolts with his foot, Clay moves to the right and looks at the side of the old man's head.

"This animatronic is amazing," he says, tapping the glass. "They even put these tiny hairs in his ear. And look at the pores on his nose, the whiskers. This thing is, like, a work of art."

Standing on the left side of the machine, Joel cups a hand around his eyes. "There's a mole on his jaw. Yeah, this is Hollywood level work. Hey, maybe it is. Maybe it's a prop from a movie that got reused for the machine, and that's why it looks different."

Both boys move back to the front, and Clay can't help but feel a slight chill from the lifelike stare of the figure in the machine. He half expects it to wink at him.

"You think it still works?" Joel asks as he circles the machine.

Clay hunches down and squints. "If it's back here, it's probably broken." On the left side, near the bottom, he notices a small brass tag bolted to the wood with the inscription "M40" engraved into the metal.

Joel comes back around to the front and stands next to Clay, the two of them staring at the frozen man.

"I just want to see it move," Joel says, absently grabbing that small metal handle. As soon as his fingers wrap around it, the crystal ball sparks to life, bathing the inside of the machine with an eerie blue light that streaks across the glass. The old man's eyes begin to glow and flicker, as if the bulbs behind his eyes struggle to remain lit. His claw hand waves mechanically back and forth above the crystal ball while a raspy voice rattles from the small speaker.

"Welcome, fellow travelers. Do you wish to see your future?"

Joel jerks his hand away from the machine and says, "Shit!"

The crystal ball continues to pulse, and maybe it's that blue light, but Clay thinks the old man's pupils have shifted slightly and are looking right at Joel.

Clay chuckles nervously. "He asked you a question. You should answer him."

Joel brushes some dust off the arm of his jacket and laughs.

"Yes," he says dramatically. "I wish to see my future."

"*I must warn you,*" the tinny metallic voice says, *"I see all. By peering into the future, we shape it. You may see what you do not wish to see. Do you still want to proceed?"*

Feeling more confident that the old man is not going to grab the crystal ball, smash through the glass, and attack him, Joel takes a step closer and says, "Yes. I do."

"Very well."

The hand waves a few more times, and the blue glow gets brighter. A mechanical hum comes from the machine, from the compartment beneath the old man's torso. The creak and squeal of gears grinding together.

A ticket appears in the slot, and the blue light suddenly goes out.

Joel flashes Clay a surprised look and an apprehensive smile, then reaches out, takes the ticket, and reads it to himself. On the side Clay can see is the word *Longsight,* written in the same elaborate script. He watches his friend's face, watches his eyes move back and forth as he reads the ticket. When Joel lowers his hand, his face is as pale as the moon.

9

"WHAT'S IT SAY?" CLAY ASKS.

Joel passes the ticket to Clay, his hand shaking a little as he does. The words are typed in a simple font, bold and clear.

ON BLACK PATHS WHERE STEEL HORSES RUN FREE
BEWARE THE ONE THAT BENDS YOUR KNEE
A STILLNESS COMES, NOT CALM, BUT STRIFE
WHERE ONCE YOU RAN, NOW YOU WILL BE BOUND FOR LIFE

Clay has to admit the message is cryptic. Dark, even. But the only reason to be nervous about what it says is if you believe in fortunes told by machines.

He laughs and hands the ticket back. "You know how these work? There's a roll of fortunes, maybe ten or twenty different ones, and the machine just cycles through all of them. If you fed it enough quarters, you'd end up getting the same fortune eventually."

Joel stares at his ticket and does not look convinced. "Why would they keep it back here if it works?"

"Probably because it gives people creepy fortunes," Clay says. "Probably freaked people out, so they decided not to use it anymore.

Joel shakes the piece of paper. "What do you think this means?"

"I don't think it means anything. Some guy came up with the fortunes and had them printed and put in the machine."

The sound of rain fills the silence between them.

"It's just a toy," Clay says. "Like horoscopes in the newspaper. It only means something if you see meaning in it."

Joel nods, still looking at his ticket.

"I'll try it," Clay says, moving closer to the machine. "We'll see what my ticket says."

He grabs the cold metal handle—he doesn't believe in the machine, but a lightning flash in his brain hopes that maybe it does work and it'll spit out a fortune that predicts a future with Harper—and squeezes, feels a slight electric shock on the skin of his palm as the crystal ball ignites once more and the raspy voice comes out of the speaker. The old man's eyes grow bright as the bulbs hidden behind the pupils flicker to life.

Do you wish to see more? The voice says.

Clay pulls his hand away and swallows.

"That's not what it said the first time," Joel whispers.

"It's a recording," Clay says. "Probably runs through a bunch of different phrases.

Then, to the machine, Clay says, "Yes." The glowing eyes appear to look right at him. He holds back a shiver.

What I see is what will be. You may try and rewrite the future, but all paths lead to what I have foreseen.

Clay turns to his friend and rolls his eyes. "Yeah, okay," he says. "Just tell me my fortune."

As you wish.

There is a mechanical whir and a ticket pokes from the slot. Clay takes it and reads it out loud.

TRAPPED INSIDE YOUR MIND'S OWN JAIL
WHAT YOU DO NOT WISH TO SEE WILL BE UNVEILED
THE DUST OF TIME, IT SHIFTS AND SWAYS
THE CLOCK TICKS UNENDING, COUNTING DOWN FOUR DAYS

His heart skips a couple of beats as he reads the words, and it feels like air is trapped in his chest. It shouldn't matter what the ticket says, but Clay is overcome with a sudden and intense sensation that it does matter. That each word is significant and meaningful, a glimpse into a future that doesn't yet exist. The floor seems unsteady under his feet, like the concrete has melted, and his leg muscles tense to remain balanced. He feels dizzy.

He tries to keep his voice steady. "See, man," Clay says, waving the ticket, "total bullshit. It doesn't even make sense."

Joel gives a fake laugh. "Yeah, total bullshit."

Clay looks beyond all the junk in the direction of the fair and sees two shapes running through the rain. "Here they come," he mutters.

"Remember what I said," Joel says.

The sight of Kenny and Harper, side by side, stings like Clay didn't know emotions could sting. It's hot needles pressing into his scalp. It's an acid bubble he can't swallow. Soon, they reach the shelter of the tent, laughing and shaking rain from their hair.

"We didn't know where you guys went," Kenny says.

"I got a bad stomachache," Joel offers, before Clay can say something stupid. "Just needed to walk it off, and then it started raining."

Harper clutches a large stuffed monkey covered in slime green hair. "Look what Kenny won for me at the bottle toss!"

Kenny brushes past Clay, ignoring him, and approaches the fortune machine.

"Longsight?" he says. "Shouldn't it be Zoltan, or Cosmos, or something cool?"

Clay catches Harper's eyes—she smiles at him sweetly, like nothing is wrong. Like she wasn't just making out with Kenny and crushing Clay's heart at the same time. All the fantasies and dreams of he and Harper together are being redrawn, painfully, in real time inside his head. His chest aches to look at her. He can't even force himself to fake a smile, and he turns away.

"It works," Clay says to Kenny. "You should try it. Just grab that handle."

He isn't sure why he suggests Kenny have his fortune told, but the strange feeling of the handle still tingles on his palm, and his head is still light from reading the ticket. He wants Kenny to feel that same disorientation. He wants to crack his confidence a little, and some deep part of him hopes he gets a terrible fortune. Something so dark and violent that it shakes him to his core. Something that makes all his charisma crumble. Maybe even something that causes Harper to see him as weak and afraid.

"Jesus," Kenny says. "That guy looks real, doesn't he? Creepy." He gets closer, face inches from the machine.

Clay fights the urge to shove the back of his head and crack his nose against the glass.

Kenny's face turns slightly, and he sees the ticket in Clay's hand. "You tried it? It works?" He reaches for the ticket, "Let me see what it says."

Clay pulls his hand away and takes two steps backward.

"Come on, man. What's it say?"

"Nothing," Clay says, taking another step. "Just bullshit."

Kenny straightens up, shoulders back. Clay blinks once, and when his eyes open, Kenny has closed the distance between them, again reaching for the ticket.

"Show me what it says."

It's his friend's insistence that makes Clay's heart thud like fear, like those white-hot seconds right before a fight. It's Kenny's sense of entitlement to take, touch, see, read what belongs to Clay.

"Is it about your love life?" Kenny says, smiling, teeth bright in the darkness of the tent.

Joel says, "Shit man, let it go."

"Does it say you're going to meet someone special tonight?" Kenny looks to Harper, then to Joel, to see if they think his joke is funny. Harper smiles, but Clay knows it's not quite real.

Clay shoves the ticket into his jacket. "Why do you care so much about what mine says? Try it yourself and get your own ticket."

Kenny thinks this over, squinting at Clay with an arrogant smile. It's the smile of someone who has had everything go his way tonight. Someone who feels, temporarily, untouchable.

He nods silently, then says, "Okay," and turns back to the machine. He reaches out one hand and wraps his fingers around the metal handle. A low hum comes out of his mouth, and his head begins shaking up and down. His voice gets higher-pitched until he sounds like he's screaming through closed lips. His whole body starts convulsing as his voice becomes a shriek.

Harper runs to his side, screaming his name. Clay reaches for her, to stop her from touching Kenny in case he's being electrocuted.

The shriek stops. His body goes still, and now there's quiet laughter. Kenny turns around to face the three friends, a big, stupid grin on his face.

"Oh, you fucker," Joel says, and laughs out of relief.

Harper slaps his arm and mutters, "You dick."

Clay has found that certain moments in life reveal hidden parts of his design. The way he reacts or feels about a situation can surprise him, and he's learned to take them seriously, to privately analyze and try to understand them. Now is one of those moments as he discovers he is disappointed Kenny is not actually hurt. Some deep, dark part wanted to see Kenny's skin melt to the metal handle, for the machine to send a thousand volts of electricity blazing through his bones, burning his blood to dust, boiling his eyes until they dripped down the crackling skin of his face. He wanted to see Kenny's heart stop.

Kenny laughs again and grabs the handle. The blue light from the crystal ball illuminates his face, and the face of the old man in the machine. Young man and old man stare at each other as the animatronic's eyes glow. The gnarled fingers caress the ball, back and forth, as a voice comes from the speaker.

"Welcome. I can see your future as clearly as if it were a photograph. Do you wish to see?"

Kenny cocks his head.

"You have to answer him," Clay says. "There's probably a microphone or something."

"Yes," Kenny says quietly. Then louder, "Yes."

He can feel it, Clay thinks. He can feel something is off about the machine.

"Sometimes it is best not to know," the voice says. *"Knowing too much can be a curse, but ignorance is bliss."*

Kenny bangs a fist into the side of the machine. "Just tell me what you see, god damn it!"

Is it Clay's imagination, or is there a tone of irritation when the voice says, *"Very well"?*

The crystal ball flashes blue light a few times, strobing Kenny's expression, his narrowed eyes and wet lips. The old man's eyes flash too, bright then dim then bright again. A storm inside the machine.

It stops suddenly, and a ticket appears in the slot. Kenny reaches for it when a strong voice shouts from behind them.

"Hey! What the hell are you kids doing back here?"

All four of them turn and see a tall, bulky man with a bald head dressed in mechanic's coveralls striding toward them.

"This area is off limits." The man points back toward the fair. "Get outta here, you little shits. I swear to God, if you broke anything…."

Kenny takes Harper's hand, her eyes go wide, and they start running, back out into the rain, the sound of Kenny's laughter echoing behind them.

"Sorry, sir," Joel yells at the man, who is still just a shape in the raindrops, approaching with slow, steady steps.

"Don't fucking 'sir' me," he yells back. "I'm calling the cops if anything's busted."

"Let's bail," Joel whispers.

Clay glances down at the machine, sees Kenny's ticket still sticking out of the slot. He snatches the paper, slips it in his pocket, then he and Joel take off running.

10

GETTING OUT OF THE FAIRGROUNDS is easy. The four friends blend in with the crowd as they make their way through the turnstiles, hiding their hands so no one can see they aren't wearing the wristbands that grant you entrance to the park. The persistent rain has packed the few indoor game venues and restaurants, while everyone else runs through puddles, covering their heads with whatever items they carry.

Out in the parking lot, Clay, Harper, Joel, and Kenny pile into Clay's car, still buzzing from their encounter with the Fright Fair employee. Nothing was broken, nothing stolen—but they feel like criminals just the same. Chased off the backlot of that eerie carnival. A place they had no business being. A place they had snuck into because they are young and reckless and believed they could get away with it. And they did, and now their nerves are crackling, and they can't shake the excitement.

Even Clay, with the dark clouds brewing in his head, smiles and laughs as they get in his car, drops of rain dripping down his face. He has to stop himself from punching the gas and tearing out of the parking lot like the cops were after them.

They relive the fun, the nervous energy of the night as Clay drives through the nearly empty streets of Medford. Kenny talks the most, as he usually does. Placing himself at the center of all that happened, even though it was Clay and Joel who discovered the machine.

"It was so creepy," Harper says.

Clay stares at her in the rearview mirror for so long he forgets to pay attention to the road, and he has to stomp the brakes to avoid running a red light, slamming them all forward and causing the seatbelts to bite into their flesh. Joel lifts his eyebrows but doesn't say anything. Harper's cheeks are flush with blood rush, her skin and eyes aglow in the traffic light, as she smiles and bounces in her seat. Clay can't see her hands, but he prays Kenny's fingers aren't intertwined with hers.

He couldn't take it. Not in his own car.

Joel sits in the passenger seat with a gentle smile on his face as he circles one fingertip through the moisture on the inside of the window.

Despite his anger toward Kenny, Clay feels a sudden surge of love toward his friends. Kenny included.

Weird, he thinks, how often the things that make others so unbearable are the very traits that make them irreplaceable. And maybe that's another part of being an adult—not looking for people without flaws but finding people whose flaws you can tolerate and live with.

Some part of Clay is annoyed with the way Kenny talks and talks, but another part of him thinks, *Let him have this moment.*

He'll go back home to an alcoholic father with a quick right hook. A house nearly creaking with the tension created by a man who hates himself even more than he hates everyone else. That Kenny can laugh at all is a small miracle. Yeah, Clay's parents fight a lot, and he doesn't think their marriage will last another three months. But he has them both, and they love him. Kenny doesn't have that, and it must shape him. In fact, Clay knows it does, and he feels ashamed for his pettiness and selfishness.

Kenny's face glows blue in the rearview mirror, like it did when he stood at the Longsight machine, as he checks the time on his phone.

"Hey," he says, leaning forward and putting a hand on Clay's shoulder. "Can you drop me off first? I know it's out of the way, but Dad wanted me home by eleven, and it's ten-fifty."

"Yeah, sure," Clay said, pressing the accelerator a few miles over the speed limit.

Seven minutes later, they pull in front of Kenny's house. He jumps out, blows everyone a kiss, and runs to the front door.

TV light flickers on the sun-bleached curtains in the living room, and Clay guesses Kenny probably changed the moment he walked through that door. The careless energy, the swagger, most likely disappeared as he crept down the hall to his room. He imagines Kenny's dad shouting a drunken question or accusation, and Kenny trying to figure out how to respond without incurring his wrath.

Like a man walking through a minefield. Every day.

Clay's shame grows as his eyes move from the house to Harper's reflection in the rearview mirror. She watches the house, too, but she doesn't know what Clay knows. Not all of it, anyway.

He thinks about what Joel had said and decides, yes, he can be happy for her. For Kenny, too. He needs to be if he doesn't want to lose them both as friends.

As he pulls away from the curb, Clay decides to drop Harper off first. He doesn't want to be alone with her. He doesn't trust himself not to say the wrong thing, and there are so many wrong things to say. Selfish words that will do nothing but cut. Words that will cause her to look at him differently. He's not okay yet, but he will be eventually.

Another adult lesson that's been growing inside him. Whatever is not okay right now will be later. Everything that hurts so much in the moment will hurt less with time.

Clay turns on the radio, and like some kind of sign, The Cranberries song "Linger" comes out of his crappy speakers. In the rearview mirror, he sees Harper gaze out the window, nodding gently in time as her lips mouth the words.

11

AFTER DROPPING HARPER OFF, IT'S just Clay and Joel. Clay turns down the radio so the music is a soft soundtrack to the rush of tires and rain. Joel yawns and leans his seat back, one hand turning the fortune machine ticket slowly.

"Listen," Clay says, "I'm not sure how else to say this, so I'll just say it. Thanks for what you said earlier about Harper and Kenny. I didn't want to hear it, but I think it helped."

Joel sits up straighter. "Yeah? I'm really glad to hear that, man. Truly."

The Corolla comes to a stop at an intersection as Clay waits for the light to turn green.

"I don't know, maybe it's that machine, or maybe it's just the night, but I've been thinking a lot about time. About the future."

Joel stops spinning the ticket. "What about it?"

The light turns green. Clay inches the car forward.

"We never know what's coming, do we? When we're in junior high, we think high school will be one way. Then, in high school, we think college will be one way. Then a job, maybe a family. But we're just guessing. Hoping."

"So much of it is out of our control," Joel says.

"Exactly. And when we think about the future, we only think of the good things we hope will happen."

Joel closes his eyes, smiles, and whispers, "Lauren Sanchez."

Clay laughs, "Yeah, and that will never happen."

Another song by a 90s British band comes on the radio. A song Clay never liked, but with the dark and the rain, with his friend in the passenger seat, it suddenly seems right. The perfect song for the moment.

"We never think about the bad stuff that's coming," Clay says. "We know it's going to, I just don't think we know how to imagine it."

"Do you think it helps to try and picture bad shit that'll happen in the future?"

Clay shrugs. "I don't know. What I do know is that we have to figure out a way to live that works when things are good and when they're bad."

Joel tightens his lips and nods. "I think maybe my dad did that. Mom taking off ripped his heart out, but he never let himself fall apart. He never…gave into it, I guess. He was strong before she left, and he's strong now. Maybe I feel strong because of him. Because I know you can live through whatever rips your heart out."

The song, a minor key tune about waiting for someone to love you back, makes sense in a way it never did before, and Clay decides he'll give the whole album a listen once he gets home.

"What made you think about all this?" Joel asks. "Was it Harper?"

Clay nods. "Yeah, that's part of it. Also, that machine. Maybe that's the point of the weird fortunes. Most say something good is gonna happen. This machine makes you think."

"Yeah," Joel says, looking out the window again, fidgeting with the ticket. "Maybe."

They pull onto the street where Joel lives, over a mile from Clay's house, but still on the bad side of town. Clay can't even keep track of how many times he's come to pick up Joel, only to find a couple police cars parked haphazardly, as the cops haul someone out of a rundown house barefoot and handcuffed.

Clay pulls into Joel's driveway. "Anyway, all that to say thanks."

Instead of getting out, Joel sits there, looking at his house.

"That machine," he says, quietly. "It made me feel weird. Did you get that? Kind of like the feeling when you think someone is hiding in the dark to scare you."

Clay swallows and nods silently.

"I still feel it," Joel says. "I know what you mean about it making you think. But I don't like what I'm thinking about."

He holds up the ticket. "I know bad stuff will happen, but I'll have plenty of time to think about it when it does. I'd rather focus on the good until then, you know?"

"Makes sense," Clay says. "Makes a lot of sense."

Joel opens the door and steps out, then turns and drops his ticket. It flutters and lands face down on the passenger seat.

With a hand on the Corolla's roof, Joel leans forward. "One other thing bothers me about that machine. It lit up, the robot moved, and a ticket came out."

"Yeah?"

"It lit up pretty bright. I checked, Clay, it wasn't plugged in."

"Maybe it ran on a battery?"

"I checked all around it. No plug, no extension cord. I just didn't like it. Not at all."

Joel stands up straight, slaps the roof once and gives Clay a grin. "Talk tomorrow, man."

Clay says, "See ya," and watches Joel jog up the steps of the porch, dig a keyring out of his front pocket, and unlock the front door. Then, remembering what tomorrow is, Clay rolls down his window. "Hey, good luck with the test drive. Let me know how it goes."

Joel gives a thumbs up and disappears inside the house.

Clay waits for a few seconds, wondering what it's like to live in a home where every single room contains memories of a person you loved and lost. If that's why humans invented ghost stories, to make sense of all those unexpected emotions lurking around every corner. He wonders if Joel ever sees his mom's outline sitting in a chair, or standing at the stove, or folding laundry. If it's hard to live with past moments flickering on the walls of your subconscious.

Once the light in Joel's room turns on, Clay backs out into the street and starts heading home. He didn't like the machine either, but the feeling was irrational, illogical. He thinks he doesn't like it because of the old man animatronic inside. It was too realistic, and that broke some kind of illusion. And now, the more he thinks about it, a battery doesn't make sense. Why hook a battery up to something stored in a tent with all the other random equipment and broken machinery? And if it was an internal battery, wouldn't the charge have died by now? Why would it still work as well as it did?

The questions make Clay feel uneasy and light-headed.

Ten minutes later, Clay parks on the street in front of his house and is surprised to see the living room lamps are on. Mom usually leaves the porch light on at night, but never the lights inside.

He picks up Joel's ticket from the passenger seat, shoves it in the pocket of his jeans, then walks along the side of the house to the very back and enters through the laundry room. He slips off his shoes and creeps toward the living room. His parents' bedroom door is open. They're still awake.

When he goes into the living room and sees Mom sitting on the couch, he knows something is wrong. Mom's eyes are red and swollen. One hand clutches a used tissue, and several others are crumpled on the cushion beside her. Dad sits in the recliner across from her. He looks tired. Worn out.

"Hey, bud," Dad says. "Take a seat. Your mom and I need to tell you something."

Clay crosses the living room in slow motion, as if walking through a forcefield that makes his legs feel made of concrete. Each breath is slow and shallow. His feet sink into the plush carpet, sliding along the fibers because he can barely lift his legs. Static electricity crackles from his fingertips as he reaches the couch and sits down. Warm water fills his ears as Mom cries and Dad tells him exactly what he expected to hear.

12

CLAY LIES AWAKE IN THE dark, staring at the ceiling. His whole body feels weighted down and his thoughts hum at a painful frequency. He's lost. Adrift. The bed is a small boat in the middle of a black ocean.

After Mom and Dad told him they were separating, Clay nodded when they asked if he understood. He nodded again when Dad said nothing would change. He kept nodding when Mom said they loved him so much and wanted what was best for him.

Then he stood and sleepwalked down the hall to his room, shut his door, and punched the wall as hard as he could, ramming his fist through the sheetrock, causing white dust to snow on the carpet. Then he climbed into bed fully clothed, blood leaking from his knuckles, but he didn't feel any pain.

He cried. He grabbed a pillow and held it to his face as the tears came. Not since he was a little kid has he cried as long and hard. Breathing in his own hot breath, screaming into the pillow until his throat was raw, punching the mattress with one fist.

TRAPPED INSIDE YOUR MIND'S OWN JAIL

Now, he waits for sleep. Prays for it.

What hurt the most were the lies. It would have been better if Dad said, "Listen, son. This is going to completely fuck up your life. Everything you've known up until now is going to change. You won't see me as much. In fact, there will be days when we don't talk and I won't know what you're going through."

Clay would have preferred Mom to say, "We love you, but it isn't enough for us to work out our problems because we're both too selfish. And you'll hear me weeping alone in the bed I used to share with your dad. The house will be so much quieter now, and you'll spend a lot of time wondering which of us is at fault. Whose side you should take. It's going to be wild, so hang on tight!"

But they could never be honest with themselves, so of course, they weren't honest with him.

Just when he thinks the initial shock and pain have worn off, another thought streaks across his mind, like a stray bullet, and punctures a hole in his approaching calm.

Sleep doesn't come for hours, and when it does, he sees the glowing face of the old man in the Longsight machine, eyes alight, claw-hand gripping the crystal ball, as a mechanical laugh issues from the speaker.

WHAT YOU DO NOT WISH TO SEE WILL BE UNVEILED

He wakes up to the creak of his bedroom door and Mom's face peeking in.

"Honey, are you awake?"

Her eyes are still swollen and red, and fresh tears are glistening on her cheeks, in the wrinkles around her mouth. He can't take another emotional display. He's still too raw to deal with someone else's pain. Clay turns his head to the bedside table and looks at the red numbers on his digital clock. It's almost noon.

Mom creaks the door open all the way, crosses the room, and sits on the edge of the bed.

She puts a hand on his shoulder. "Honey, you need to wake up."

"I'm awake," Clay says. "What do you want?"

Mom tries to speak, stifles a sob. "It's Joel…"

Clay quickly sits up, alert. His heart slams against his ribs like a hammer on a nail. "What about him? Is he okay?"

"He…he was in a bad car accident this morning."

"Oh fuck. Oh shit."

"He's in the hospital right now, in a coma. He'll be going into surgery soon, but it looks like he has a spinal cord injury, and the doctors aren't sure if he'll ever walk again."

Clay jumps off the bed, presses his hands to his face, and starts pacing the room. "Oh my god," he whispers again and again, a sudden mantra.

"I'm so sorry, honey," Mom says, reaching for him, but her hand just hangs there in the distance between them. "I know it's a lot."

Her voice is underwater, filtered through miles of black ocean. Clay falls to his knees and feels around the floor under his bed until he finds his cellphone. He opens it up to text Harper, to text Kenny, but then he stops.

Joel's ticket.

His fingers dig into the front pocket of his jeans. He feels the paper and pulls. Two tickets fall out. He forgot he also had Kenny's ticket. Still kneeling, Clay turns them both over until he finds Joel's and he reads it again, eyes growing wider, mouth falling open.

What seemed so confusing at the time now makes perfect sense.

ON BLACK PATHS WHERE STEEL HORSES RUN FREE
BEWARE THE ONE THAT BENDS YOUR KNEE
A STILLNESS COMES, NOT CALM, BUT STRIFE
WHERE ONCE YOU RAN, NOW YOU WILL BE BOUND FOR LIFE

13

CLAY LEAVES HIS MOTHER CRYING on his bed and marches to the laundry room, slips on his shoes, grabs his jacket and keys, and slams the back door on his way out. The sky is filled with dark clouds. and the streets are slick with rain. A heavy mist hangs in the air, making the day feel paused at some darker, earlier hour.

Clay gets in the car and starts it, flips the heat on all the way, and waits for the windows to defog. The scent of Harper's perfume still hangs in the air, a faint, ghostly presence coming from the backseat.

He fights the urge to cry again as his hands grip the steering wheel. He fights the urge to pray. Because, after all, if a carnival machine was able to foresee Joel's accident, and God did nothing to stop it from happening, what good will praying do anyway?

14

AFTER TEXTING KENNY, CLAY SPEEDS over to his house and finds him sitting on the curb with a cigarette between his fingers. Kenny's dad buys cigarettes by the case, so he hasn't noticed yet that Kenny steals a few from each new pack. He takes one last drag, flicks the butt into the street, and climbs in the car.

"Fuck," he says. "Have you heard anything else?"

Clay shakes his head.

"We picking up Harper?"

"Her mom is dropping her off at French Press."

They drive in silence as the defroster works even harder to clear the windows, now that Kenny is in the car.

"Shit," Kenny says, and bangs a fist against the door. "Shit." He buries his face in his hands and growls like an animal. A wounded creature who feels pain but can't understand why it happens. "This doesn't even seem real," he says.

"Rain," Clay says, gripping the wheel extra tight and keeping his eyes on the road. "Going too fast, maybe. Hit a puddle, hydroplaned, and slammed into a power pole."

"Fuck."

A few minutes later, Clay parks at the French Press, not far from a white Mercedes SUV. Harper gives a small wave from the passenger seat and gets out. Her mom exits the vehicle as well and gives the boys a quick hug. Her eyes are as red and swollen as Clay's mom's. For a quick second, Clay wonders if Harper ever worries her mom and dad are going to divorce, or if the big house, expensive cars, and designer furniture insulate them from the pain of normal people. To him, they are citizens of another world, and he wonders if they ever view the tiny planet he lives on—a sphere of dirt, grime, heartache, addiction, and financial stress—with disdain and scientific curiosity.

"If you see Joel's dad, please let him know we're thinking of him and I'll drop a meal off at the house later," Harper's mom says to Clay.

"I will."

When she gets back in the Mercedes and drives away, the three friends head into French Press, order coffee, and find a corner table near a window. Harper's nose is running and she keeps wiping it with a tissue. He wants to comfort her, but it's Kenny who gently holds her hand. To his surprise, Clay doesn't even care. Not today.

It's as if he is on stage, acting in a play, and his role is to be in the background. In shadow. Away from the spotlight. His problems and worries shrink in the glare of something much bigger.

Harper rests her head against Kenny's shoulder and sniffs. "I told my mom we might visit him later," she says.

Kenny nods. "We have to. Even if he doesn't know we're there, we have to see him. Maybe he'll still be able to hear us."

A barista approaches their table, balancing three paper cups of steaming coffee. She sets them down without a word, but she gives Clay a sad smile as she retreats behind the counter.

Minutes pass as Harper and Kenny discuss the accident, how it happened, and how sick Joel's dad must feel.

"It was the first time he drove the car," Kenny says to Clay. "Remember? Test drive today."

"I remember," Clay says, taking a sip of his coffee. It's still so hot it burns his tongue.

He looks up and catches Harper staring at him. Her eyes are extra blue, shimmering with tears.

"You're quiet," she says. "You okay?"

He almost tells them about his parents, about the nuclear bomb they dropped on him last night, but he can't. Instead, he nods slowly and reaches into his pocket, producing Joel's wrinkled ticket from the Longsight machine. He sets it on the table, face up, so they can read what it says.

Kenny's eyes scramble back and forth as the skin between his eyes folds into a crease. Harper's free hand goes to her mouth.

"What the fuck is this?" Kenny says, looking at Clay now.

"You know what it is."

"How?" Harper says.

Anger creeps into Kenny's voice. "This isn't right, man. This is fucked up."

Clay focuses his words on Harper, because he knows she'll listen.

"That machine we found, Joel tried it first, and this is what came out. We didn't see it then, but now, it's pretty clear exactly what it means."

Harper's hair swings back and forth past her chin as she shakes her head. Strands of hair stick to her cheeks where tears are still wet.

"This doesn't make any sense."

"No, it doesn't," Clay says. "Unless—"

"Unless what?" Kenny interrupts.

Clay swallows and smooths out the ticket with his fingers, so the words are clear. "Unless the machine works, and it sees what's coming."

"No, no, no," Kenny says, emphasizing each word with a shake of his head. "How? How is that even possible?"

Clay lifts and slams his hand down on the table, causing their cups to jump and splash coffee. "How is not the question," Clay almost yells. "It doesn't matter how it's possible, Kenny. What matters is that the machine predicted Joel's accident twelve hours before it happened. It predicted he wouldn't be able…he wouldn't be able to…."

Clay tries to stop the tears, to blink them back, but he can't. "Where once you ran, now you're bound for life. Where is he right now? In a hospital bed, tied down by wires. Read the fucking ticket, Kenny. Look at it. Yeah, it's vague until you know exactly what it's talking about."

Kenny snorts, gives a cocky "this is all bullshit smile," and looks out the window. Clay picks up the ticket and holds it right in front of Kenny's face, forcing him to look at it.

"It has to be a coincidence, right?" Harper says. "Realistically. Say something vague on the ticket, and the person can make it mean anything."

"Black paths means roads," Clay says. "Steel horses are cars. A stillness comes, that's a coma. What else does that sound like?"

"Jesus, man," Kenny says, finally looking back at Clay. "You don't have to get so pissed about it."

"I'm not pissed. I'm worried."

"Worried about what? Joel's accident already happened."

Clay drops Joel's ticket and reaches into his pocket. He places Kenny's ticket on the table. The ticket he'd carried since last night but didn't read until this morning, waiting for his car to warm up.

"What is this?" Kenny asks, but he knows exactly what it is. Clay sees it in his wild eyes. The fear.

He remembers what it says.

15

A LITTLE SPARK, A TOXIC, CARELESS BREATH
A ROLLING DARK CLOUD, A DREAM OF DEATH
IT SNEAKS WHILE YOU SLUMBER, THE WEB HAS BEEN SPUN
WHAT ONCE STOOD PROUDLY WILL BE WRECKAGE BEFORE THE RISING SUN

16

THE TICKET RENDERS BOTH KENNY and Harper unable to speak. At first, Kenny tries to hide it from her, but she snatches it from him and reads it. Her hands tremble as she reads the words. Her eyes grow wide, and her chin quivers.

Clay feels guilty for bringing it out in front of her, but he also knows Kenny won't listen to him if they are alone. Kenny needs to see Harper's reaction to take it seriously. But after that, Kenny won't even look at Clay, like his friend had somehow betrayed him.

Kenny is silent all the way to the hospital. He sits in the back, next to Harper, as Clay drives through the misty afternoon. His phone buzzes on the passenger seat as the words "Dad Cell" fill the screen. He ignores the call and keeps driving.

After parking at the hospital, Harper and Kenny walk toward the sliding glass doors holding hands. Clay trails behind them, still carrying both tickets in his pocket.

He wishes he knew what to say.

Do adults know? Yesterday, he would have said, "Yes." But after his parents destroyed what little peace he had, after they lied and said the same exact bullshit you'd hear on a made-for-TV movie, Clay isn't so sure adults know what to say when the moment is tense, when the information is hard. No one likes to cause pain, he knows that much. But he also thinks some adults understand that things can't be right all the time, and they lean into it. They speak with honesty.

This isn't okay. This isn't right. But we have to face what it is, not what we wish it could be.

They leave the cold air and enter the stifling, sterile warmth of the hospital. Kenny stops at the information desk and asks where Joel's room is, then they follow signs and arrows that lead to the ICU.

Standing outside room 9, no one moves.

Kenny turns to Clay and says, "I'm sorry I got mad. I'm not mad at you. Or, I shouldn't be. I'm just… confused."

Clay puts a hand on his friend's shoulder, thinks that's all it will be, but then he pulls him closer into an embrace and holds him for longer than either of them has ever hugged each other.

When Kenny pulls away, tears are running down his face. He gives an embarrassed smile and takes Harper's hand. She's crying too.

Clay knocks on the door.

It's opened by Ray, Joel's dad, a slight man a little shorter than Clay with a kind face and normally bright eyes. Except today they're red with veins and filled with tears that quiver in the overhead lights. He's dressed in a blue flannel, jeans, and well-worn work boots. He works as an electrician, and Joel has talked about how he plans to someday apprentice with his father, maybe even start their own business.

Ray begins crying as soon as he sees Joel's friends, and he hugs them all, one by one, whispering, "Thank you for coming. How are you doing? You hanging in there?"

Harper breaks down, mascara streaming from her eyes as Ray takes both of her hands in his and says, "Oh, honey, it's so hard, I know."

Clay sees Joel's body over Ray's shoulder, sees his friend lying in bed, motionless. A tube leads from Joel's mouth to a machine on wheels that makes a sound like breathing. Joel's chest rises with each mechanical inhale. His face is covered in dozens of small bloody holes from when the windshield shattered and sprayed glass bullets throughout the car. A thick laceration extends from the corner of his mouth to the edge of his ear, stitched closed but still leaking blood. The bridge of his broken nose is crooked, and the skin under each eye is shiny and red.

WHAT YOU DO NOT WISH TO SEE WILL BE UNVEILED

I don't want to see this, Clay thinks. *This is my ticket. And all these images will be trapped inside my mind's jail for the rest of my life. A life sentence of seeing Joel in this bed.*

Clay approaches the bed and puts his hand on Joel's. A thick, padded bracelet that resembles a handcuff is strapped around his wrist.

Ray appears at his side. "They do that in case he wakes up. So he doesn't try to pull the tube out."

Both of Joel's legs look like they've been beaten with a baseball bat. Swollen, bruised flesh. Yellow, purple, and angry. Fresh incisions curve around his thighs, held together with dozens of sparkling metal staples.

"The bones were shattered," Ray says, one hand on his son's leg, the other on Clay's back. "The surgeon pieced him back together with rods, plates, and screws, but there's nothing he can do about the spinal injury."

He chokes back a sob. "I'm just so grateful to God that he's alive." His watery eyes look into Clay's. "I was supposed to go on that drive with him," he says. "Did you know that?"

Clay nods.

"I got offered some overtime. Joel told me to take the shift, said we'd drive together later today." He shakes his head, like he can't believe it. Can't believe how a single phone call might have saved his life, just like how a single ticket from a fortune-telling machine might have destroyed his son's.

17

AS THEY DRIVE AWAY FROM the hospital, Clay now watches
Kenny in the rearview mirror instead of Harper. At every
red light, every stop sign, Clay glances at that oval-shaped
piece of glass and observes his friend. When Kenny
smiles at Harper, it's a cautious expression because of the
puffy flesh under his left eye, faintly blue, tender.

Shame hits Clay again. Shame that he could feel
jealous of someone who had to fight so hard just to be
okay.

As if Kenny's happiness could only come at the ex-
pense of Clay's. A stupid way to think, sure, but teenage
boys are famous for being stupid, and that's exactly how
Clay feels. Stupid and small. A tiny speck adrift on a mas-

sive ocean filled with all the things he doesn't know. The things he can't understand.

Harper's phone buzzes, and she taps a reply, then says, "My mom wants me to come home, but she says you guys can stay for dinner if you want."

Kenny agrees, but Clay decides to pass on the invitation.

It's already starting to get dark by the time Clay pulls up to Harper's house. She gives him a hug by wrapping one arm around him. She whispers, "Take care of yourself," and gets out of the car.

Kenny says to her, "I'll be right there," and waits until she closes the door.

"I know what you're thinking," he says.

Clay tries to laugh. "When have you ever known?"

Kenny tilts his head back and stares at the upholstery of the roof. He lifts a hand and runs his fingers along the tiny black scars left by a previous owner's cigarette ashes.

"I've been thinking about the ticket all day," he says, "and I have no idea what it means."

Clay twists in his seat so he can see Kenny.

"Maybe you can just stay at your house for a few days, pretend to be sick or something, until we can figure this out."

Kenny laughs once, then winces. "Figure what out? Just because these tickets say some creepy shit does not mean they're making it happen. Joel was going to drive the car no matter what his ticket said. You already know that because you're smarter than me. Besides, every bad thing that's ever happened to me has happened at my house."

"I just think you should be safe."

"What's safe, Clay? When are we ever safe?"

Clay falls silent and lowers his eyes.

"You okay?" Kenny asks.

Even though he feels a little shitty bringing it up, he needs to tell his friend. He needs to say the words out loud, because he hasn't yet.

"My parents are getting divorced."

Kenny immediately leans forward and puts a hand on Clay's arm, squeezes. "Shit, man. I'm so sorry. That... that fucking sucks. You just find out last night?"

Clay nods, opens his mouth to speak, then stops and takes a deep breath. He needs to say the other words out loud, too. Because he hasn't said those yet either. "I'm scared, Kenny. I'm scared there's more to this than coincidence, and I don't want anything to happen to you."

Kenny gives a half-smile. "I don't want anything to happen to me either."

"I'm serious."

"So am I. Look, man. I don't know what else I can do except be careful and live my life. I'm already afraid all the time, and it takes just about all I've got to stop it from taking over my thoughts. What happened to Joel is the shittiest thing imaginable, but that doesn't mean anything will happen to me."

"Please, just be careful."

"I will."

"Promise me."

Kenny looks right into Clay's eyes and says, "I promise."

He squeezes Clay's arm one more time, opens the car door, and gets out. Harper waits on the porch, arms folded against the cold.

"Hey," Kenny says. "You sure you don't want to have dinner with us?"

"No, I need a little time alone."

"Alright. Love ya, man."

The door closes, and Clay watches as Kenny walks up to the porch. Harper opens the front door, and they stand there, together, framed in a rectangle of light. A warm house and love are waiting on the other side.

18

AS HE'S DRIVING HOME, CLAY'S mom calls. He doesn't answer because he doesn't know what to say. A minute later, his phone alerts that there's a voicemail. At a red light, he opens the phone and presses play.

"Hey, hon, it's me. I... uh... just wanted to let you know I'm not home right now. I'm actually going to grab a bite with Gina. Your dad is at the house and he's... um... he's packing up a few things, so maybe just give him the time he needs, okay? Later tonight, let's you and I curl up on the couch, watch a movie, and eat a ton of ice cream. We can talk if you need to, or we can just be together. Whatever you want. Okay, love you. And please let Ray know I'm praying for him and Joel."

There's really nowhere else Clay wants to be except home, in his room, lying in bed, and listening to music. But now, even home is hazardous.

He slams his hand into the steering wheel. The blast of sharp, sudden pain jolts his brain into a state of alertness. He hits the wheel again, gritting his teeth as his bones scrape together.

Kenny had said, "Figure out what?" and Clay wasn't sure at the time. How do you fight against something that can see into the future and print it on a ticket?

Clay has no idea, but he's going to try to find out where the machine came from. He flips on his blinker and makes a left turn, speeding toward the library downtown.

19

THE MEDFORD PUBLIC LIBRARY IS one of the newest and most modern-looking buildings in the city—two stories of slate-gray stone and large windows. Clay hasn't been here in far too long, but he still has a library card, which he needs to log on to one of the computers.

He could use his phone, but he doesn't want to sit in his car, and the monitors make everything bigger, easier to see. And he doesn't want to miss anything.

The library is mostly empty. Quiet and oddly peaceful. Clay finds an open station near a window and punches in his card number. After opening an internet browser, he sits back and stares at the blank search bar.

Where does he start?

Clay types "Longsight" and hits Enter. Most of the results only show the words "long" and "sight" separated. A couple of articles reference a man with the last name Longsight, and others seem to be related to a brand of telescope.

Nothing stands out.

He clicks over to images, hoping to see a photograph of the fortune-telling machine. He knows there are groups out there obsessed with vintage Americana—antique souvenirs, pinball machines, carnival memorabilia, and toys—but not a single image of the machine. He scrolls all the way to the bottom of one page, clicks on the next, and scrolls some more.

Nothing.

Clay sighs and rubs his tired eyes. Outside, night falls.

He clicks back to the first page and decides to scroll again, looking for anything that stands out.

Halfway down are two black-and-white photographs of the same man. One photo shows him in a classroom, standing in front of a large blackboard covered in chalk writing. He wears a suit and tie, his gray hair combed neatly, as he points at something on the board.

The image next to it appears to be a yearbook photo.

Clay's heart opens and seems to pump in slow, heavy beats. His ears sound filled with fluid. His mouth goes instantly dry.

The man in the photograph is the same in the Longsight machine. A little younger, perhaps, but there's no mistaking the face.

The teacher's name is Henry Longsight.

With shaking hands, Clay types "Henry Longsight" in the search bar and finds multiple articles about the man who taught high school history for over twenty years in Cincinnati, Ohio before vanishing in 1974.

20

CLAY RUSHES OVER TO THE nearest librarian's desk and asks how he can print articles from the computer. A kind woman with thick glasses and a curly bob swishes over to his computer station and shows him how. She reminds him, sweetly, that each page costs five cents to print, and tells him to hurry because the library will be closing soon.

Within seconds, a large printer whirs to life and begins spitting out paper. Clay clicks from one article to the next. His eyes skim the material, capturing certain words and phrases that give him a frantic energy, like he's had too much caffeine. He sees pieces of a larger puzzle scattered throughout the articles. He hits print again and again. Soon, a large stack weighs down the tray.

After checking the time on his phone, Clay scoops up all the paper and carries it to the desk, where he takes his debit card from his wallet and pays the fee.

Once he's sitting in his car, Clay texts Kenny and Harper.

I found him. I know who the man is in the machine!

Harper replies immediately with OMG!!!

Then another text, Mom and I dropped Kenny off at home about an hour ago. We should videochat and you can tell us what you found!

Kenny doesn't respond. Clay doesn't think anything of it until after he gets home to his empty house. He knows if he were to go into his parents' bedroom and look in the closet, he'd find Dad's half completely empty. He knows the three dresser drawers Dad uses will be empty, too. Dad's side of the bathroom will be cleared of his toothbrush, deodorant, razor, and shaving cream. His cologne, which Clay sometimes uses, will be gone too.

But Clay doesn't look. He doesn't want to. He goes straight to his room, closes the door, flicks on the lamp by his bed, and starts reading everything he'd printed.

He sends Kenny another text.

You won't believe what I found!

Followed by, Call me when you get this, okay?

Stretched out on his bed, Clay flips through sheets of paper, reading and re-reading the various articles. Only one was dated after 1974, the year Henry Longsight disappeared, and a single line stood out to Clay.

"I hope he found whatever he was looking for."

The distant sound of sirens comes from outside, a mournful wail that rises and falls.

One article contains a black and white photo of Longsight. Even though it is blurred with age, the severe expression and intense eyes are unmistakable. The sight of it makes Clay shiver, but he forces himself to stare at it.

Another siren, even closer this time.

Clay checks his phone, hoping for a reply from Kenny. Nothing.

It starts with the sensation of a spider crawling up the back of his neck, then it becomes tiny needle pricks along his scalp. Soon, the skin on Clay's face grows hot. He feels sweat gathering in his armpits, soaking into his shirt.

The sirens wail.

He checks his phone again and pushes the green button to call Kenny. It rings while yet another siren, this one longer and lower than the others, races down his street.

Kenny's voice comes through the speaker, and Clay is so relieved he almost yells, until he realizes it's his friend's voicemail.

"Fuck!"

Clay swings his legs off the bed and marches through the house until he reaches the front door. There is something in the air, something that stings his eyes and makes his throat tight.

He jogs down to the sidewalk and notices he is not the only one outside.

Part of the sky glows. Two blocks west, a reddish-orange haze flickers on the clouds. Houses on either side of the street are colored with the strobing lights of two police cars, an ambulance, and a firetruck.

Clay starts jogging, then running. He crosses an intersection without even bothering to look for cars.

He's whispering, praying out loud to God, the universe, to anyone who will listen.

"No, no. Please, no!"

Up until he reaches the closest police car, Clay hopes he's wrong. He hopes his burning eyes are seeing a mirage, a hallucination, but it's bright and real and vivid, and it's everything he was afraid of.

The fire truck is parked in front of Kenny's house, a thick hose attached to the nearest hydrant sprays a stream of water at an inferno. The entire house is engulfed in flames. A large section of the roof has already caved in, and the fire roars as wood cracks from inside. Black smoke billows into the sky, bending with an unfelt breeze and drifting across the neighborhood.

Clay darts around the emergency vehicle, blinking against the smoke, eyes desperately searching for Kenny or his dad. All he sees are men in uniform, firefighters in yellow suits and helmets. A female paramedic points at Clay as he wanders between all the vehicles with their flashing lights. He starts screaming his friend's name until the paramedic rushes up to him, grabs him by the shirt, and drags him away from the blaze.

Neighbors are gathered in the street, dressed in pajamas and sweatpants, bundled against the cold, shaking their heads.

"Do you know who lives here?" the paramedic asks.

Clay can't breathe. He's never had a panic attack, but everything he's heard tells him he's having one. His lungs won't accept air. His vision narrows. He hears himself say, "Kenny. My friend Kenny and his dad. He wouldn't answer. I called and texted, and he always answers, so I ran down here."

Clay breaks free of the woman's grasp, runs over to the ambulance, and looks inside. Empty. "Did you see him?" Clay asks. "Did someone take him to the hospital?"

The paramedic's blonde hair is pulled back in a ponytail. She looks at Clay with uncertainty. "Do you think he was in the house?"

Clay closes his eyes and nods. It's stupid, but the paramedic is beautiful, and Clay doesn't want her to see him cry.

She puts a hand on his shoulder. "I'm so sorry. I wish I knew the right thing to say. I'm just…I'm so sorry. We didn't see anyone, and none of the neighbors have either. In fact, we don't even know how the fire started."

Clay opens his eyes to a hellish world of smoke and fire. He's choking on the particles of burning wreckage, inhaling the house, and his friend, as they are deconstructed. He watches smoke pour out of the house and thinks of Kenny's body trapped inside, devoured, consumed, and spewed into the atmosphere.

Clay wanders a little closer, squinting at the bright flames. The paramedic stays close by, ready to grab him again should he try to run closer to the house. The firefighters hold and aim the hose at the base of the flames.

His eyes fill with tears. He wipes them away with one hand and glances down at the ground. He sees something on the asphalt, something white and orange with a blackened tip.

He kneels and picks it up.

A LITTLE SPARK, A TOXIC, CARELESS BREATH
A ROLLING DARK CLOUD, A DREAM OF DEATH

"I know how the fire started," he says, and shows the cigarette butt to the paramedic. The cigarette Kenny had stolen from his father and smoked while he sat on the curb and waited for Clay earlier that morning.

21

ASH SNOWS FROM THE SKY.

Clay watches his friend's house burn.

The once blue siding turns black as it is incinerated. The street is now full of people, held back by a line of police officers. No matter how much water is sprayed at the fire, the flames never get any smaller. The inferno is endlessly hungry, endlessly growing, and Clay knows it will not be satisfied until there is nothing left to devour.

Another thing I don't want to see. Another prisoner of my mind's jail, screaming through the bars.

He stands in a trance—awash in waves of heat, skin feeling sunburnt, swaying on his feet—when he hears his name being called. He turns to see his mother walking unsteadily down the middle of the street, clip-clopping in high heels.

"Clay, honey. Clay!"

He stumbles toward her and falls into her arms. She grips him tight, hands and fingers searching his face, his hair, his neck and back. Looking for an injury, a burn.

"Honey, what happened?"

He smells the alcohol on her breath. Cocktails with friends to try and numb the pain of her marriage falling apart.

Clay tries to answer, but only sobs.

"Are Kenny and his dad okay? Did they make it out?"

Clay shakes his head against his mother's collarbone. "They're both gone."

"Oh my god," Mom says, and begins to cry. Her other hand covers her mouth. "Oh my god. Honey, I'm sorry I wasn't here. I'm so sorry."

With the heat pushing on his back, Clay closes his eyes and still sees the angry light of the flames flickering behind his eyelids.

Time passes. Neighbors weep. Wood snaps and falls in a shower of sparks. The gush of the hose sounds like a waterfall.

Eventually, Mom whispers in Clay's ear, "Let's go home," and together they stagger back down the street to their house.

After a long shower to wash off the scent of smoke, Clay gets in bed and calls Harper. She answers, and as soon as he hears her voice, Clay begins crying.

"He's gone, Harper," he sobs. "Kenny is gone."

She goes silent for only a second, then she whispers, "No, no, no." Then she breaks down and weeps, struggling to breathe as her voice keeps repeating, "Oh God, no!"

Clay stays on the line with her, crying silently himself, occasionally offering comfort, until she's worn out. She sets down the phone and blows her nose, then asks Clay how he's doing. He has so much to say, but his mind is exhausted. All his thoughts feel like fragments, like pieces of paper with scorched edges.

They agree to meet the next day under the overpass at the bike path that runs through Hawthorne Park. After they end the call, Clay sets his phone to "do not disturb" mode. If something else bad happens during the night, he doesn't want to know until morning.

He turns off the light, closes his eyes, and tries not to picture Kenny burning to death. Tries not to imagine his flesh boiling off his bones.

The only comfort is that the ticket said he would be asleep, and Clay prays that is true.

22

WHEN HE WAKES UP, CLAY showers again because he still smells like smoke. As the warm water cascades over his head, he realizes the odor of charred wood and carpet is *inside* him, collected in his sinuses and cannot be washed off. With a shudder and sudden urge to vomit, Clay wonders if he has breathed in tiny particles of his friend, if Kenny's ashes are now carried through his bloodstream.

Mom is still sleeping, so Clay makes a pot of coffee, pours some into a travel mug, and leaves a note on the counter that says, "I love you. Meeting up with Harper. Be home later."

Clay drives through the mist to Hawthorne Park. A lone white Mercedes waits in the parking lot. He pulls up next to it and gets out.

Harper's mom comes around and gives Clay a hug, her eyes full of tears. She holds him by the shoulders, face close to his, and asks, "How are you?"

Clay struggles to not look away from the hurt in her eyes.

Another lesson. Being an adult means not turning away from the things that hurt. It means allowing yourself to see and understand the hurt in others. This woman, her heart aches in multiple ways as a mother. She hurts for her daughter's loss of a friend, and she grieves as the mother of a teenager.

"I'm okay," Clay says. "Still in shock, I guess."

He says the words even though he isn't certain they're true. They just sound like a thing people say to avoid digging into the details.

Harper's mom nods as a tear slips from one eye. "If you need anything, you and your mom, please let me know."

"I will," Clay says.

Harper gives her mother a hug goodbye, then waits until the Mercedes has vanished into the mist before throwing herself into Clay's arms and weeping.

An hour later, they sit under the overpass with the stack of paper Clay had printed at the library. They've already exhausted themselves talking about Kenny, his death, and the prediction of the Longsight machine.

This slanted section of concrete that looks over the bike path, and the cold twisting water of Bear Creek, was the place where Kenny liked to smoke a cigarette before school. Clay and Harper and Joel had spent countless hours here with their friend as he sat hunched, knees to his chin, smoking and watching the water. Deeper in thought than anyone who only saw him at school would think he was capable of.

Clay flips through the stack until he comes to the picture of Henry Longsight.

"He was a college professor," Clay says. "He taught Greek history and mythology at a small college in Illinois until he disappeared in 1974."

Clay explains that Longsight was a beloved teacher, known for his engaging style, kindness, and the way he made history come alive as he told stories of ancient times. Obsessed with ancient history, Longsight often intertwined the mythology of the gods with what was known from the archaeological record, helping his students understand how vital these beliefs were to Greek culture.

Into his teaching, Longsight incorporated slides of city ruins, temples, and artist renderings of what these places might have looked like before time eroded them.

Clay shows Harper an archived essay written by Longsight in 1968, which was published in an issue of the *Fracassi Journal of Hellenic Studies*. In it, Longsight argues that scholars dismiss the notion of Greek gods at their own peril. He wrote, "We display our true ignorance when we regard ancient civilizations as intellectually primitive compared to the modern era. There is enduring value in examining ancestral belief systems—not merely as artifacts of cultural history, but as potential indicators of modes of engagement with the unseen or the supernatural that may elude modern understanding. A connection to things we cannot see."

Clay tells Harper there were twelve primary gods responsible for various aspects of daily life.

A goddess of love, of war, of harvest. A god of the sea, of nature, of archery and music. A goddess of women, and a god of wisdom.

This was Longsight's passion up until the year 1970 when he lost his beloved wife to cancer, and later that year, his young son Henry Junior when he was struck by a car while riding his bike one winter afternoon. From this moment on, Longsight changed. His once characteristic energy vanished. He was often somber and morose during class. Even his lectures shifted focus.

Clay shuffles to another article written by Henry Longsight but rejected by multiple journals. It was later discovered in his desk after the professor's disappearance.

The essay is titled: "Reconsidering the Oracle of Delphi—Mouthpiece of Apollo."

The Oracle of Delphi, Clay explains, was a priestess who would receive "the breath of god" from a sacred spring located in a cave, and she would then act as a conduit for Apollo, the god of prophecy. Men, women, kings, and generals would travel to meet with the Oracle and seek her counsel in all things. No decision for the kingdom was made, no battle plan enacted, without her consultation and advice.

She often spoke in riddles and verse, using dense phrases pregnant with meaning that were difficult to interpret. The Oracle was considered infallible, and failure only occurred when her prophecy was misunderstood or misinterpreted.

In 1971, the year after Longsight lost his wife and son, he took an extended sabbatical to Greece. When asked about his purpose, Longsight told a fellow professor that he was going to locate the device used by the Oracle to divine the future.

This professor, confused, said, "Device?"

Longsight explained how he compared various translations of ancient Greek texts and had uncovered an error in a passage regarding how the Oracle received visions. The later, and commonly referenced translations used the word *vlepo*, meaning "to see." However, in the earliest version, *vlepo* is used in conjunction with the word *diskio*, meaning "tablet or sign."

He said, "Moses received the stone tablets inscribed with the Ten Commandments; in time, the Israelites preserved them within the Ark of the Covenant. The Aztecs revered the Sun Stone as a cosmological guide and ritual calendar. Across civilizations, one observes a recurrent pattern: the divine will made legible through physical, often monumental, artifacts. These objects serve not merely as religious symbols but as tangible mediators between the sacred and the human realm."

According to pages from his journal, which he took with him to Greece, Longsight believed the Oracle drank water from the sacred cave spring, contaminated with minerals and gases, to induce a state of altered consciousness. This state was not to commune with Apollo, but rather to protect her psyche from the visions she would have once she used a device given to her by the god. A disk-shaped machine of metal and stone that relayed to her visions of the future. Had the Oracle not been under the influence of hallucinogenic properties from the cave, the visions would have driven her mad.

Longsight was only supposed to be on sabbatical for six weeks, but he journeyed in Greece for nearly four months before returning home. By that time, he had lost interest in teaching and refused to work despite repeated requests from the college, and soon the professor found himself without a family or a job. He isolated himself in his house, converting the garage into a workshop, where he toiled day and night until he vanished.

When a neighbor had not seen him leave the house for over two weeks, she called the police to check on him. What they discovered in the garage were the remnants of a project undertaken by a fevered mind.

In one corner was a small mountain of metal ten-gallon drums, all of which were empty and had seemed to contain nothing but water.

A table saw sat at the center of the room, surrounded by large piles of sawdust. Side by side along one wall were six rectangular boxes, each the height of a man, divided at waist level by a piece of wood with a hole cut in the center. A small door on the side could allow a man to crawl inside and stand upright. There were eight completed boxes, and evidence of many more that had been torn apart and thrown into a pile in the corner. The detective in charge of the case estimated Longsight was reusing these pieces as he constructed more "upright coffins."

"Look," Clay says, pointing to a page. "Here's a picture of one."

Harper leans in, squinting.

"What does that look like to you?" Clay asks.

"Like an unfinished fortune-telling machine."

Clay nods and flips to another page. "This is from his journal. It was found on a table in the garage and later scanned into an archive by an old professor friend at the college. Look."

Clay angles the paper so Harper can see Longsight's nearly illegible handwriting scrawling across the page.

It reads:

M18 through M23 – Failures, all.

M24 – Became overcome with dizziness, faint visions of light, nothing discernible. The water helps the mind.

M31 – Heard a voice and felt someone breathing beside my ear, body tingled as though electrified.

M34 – tunnel vision, an actual tunnel made with storm clouds, light at the far end, saw a figure standing there, could not make out any features. Water is getting low.

M36 – First clear vision of an event, a flash of fire and screaming, then my body felt frozen as though it were a statue.

M38 – Closer now. I must focus on a particular question, this has been the key, I cannot approach the device with anything less than clear intention. My body felt even heavier this time, and I could not move for several minutes after the vision. I used less water to preserve what I have left., This made the experience nearly overwhelming. I slept the rest of the day afterward.

M39 – First evident and sustained vision, a moment outside time that has not yet occurred. I believe one more model with some final revisions will be the one that works as it should. Could not move for what might have been several hours. I could not lift my hands to check my watch. By the time my legs worked again, it was night. I've run out of water.

Harper looks to Clay, confused. "What does the M and a number mean?"

Clay points at the paper, his index finger tapping a word in the last sentence. "Model. Trial and error. He numbered each model, each failure, as he got closer to his goal. After his disappearance, his house and everything in it were sold at an estate sale. I think someone saw the final box and thought it was a half-finished fortune-telling machine. They probably painted it, added a few details and sold it to the fair."

Harper sighs and wraps her arms around her knees. "I wish we had a cigarette."

Clay can't sit any longer. He stands and paces on the bike path, the quiet static of the creek echoing off the overpass.

"On the machine at the fair, there's a metal tag near the bottom that says 'M40.'"

Harper stands too, and wipes dirt from her bottom. She walks carefully down the incline until she's at the edge of the embankment that leads to the creek.

"Okay," she says, her nose red and running from the cold. "So, the fortune machine was built by a crazy professor. I still don't understand, Clay. I don't understand any of this."

Fingers sore from holding the thick stack of paper, Clay waves a few pages in her direction. "Model number 40. He was close with 39, but model 40 is the one that worked."

"What do you mean it worked?" Harper says, narrowing her eyes.

Clay steps close to her, briefly feeling the old lust, the desire to hold her body close to his. He shakes his head to scatter his thoughts. "Longsight went to Greece looking for something," he says.

"A device, yeah," Harper says.

"I think he found whatever the ancient oracles used to see into the future, and he brought it back with him, along with water from that sacred cave to protect his mind as he tested each model. Toward the end, he ran out of the sacred water and probably fried his brain. Maybe he forgot who he was and he just wandered off. He tried to create a machine that would duplicate the…I don't know, environment or conditions the Oracles had that helped them use the device."

Clay puts a hand on his friend's arm and waits until her eyes meet his.

"I think he found it and he made it work," Clay says. "And I think the Oracle's disk is inside that machine."

23

HARPER STARES AT CLAY UNTIL her eyes narrow and her lips twist. She jerks her arm away from his hand and takes a step back.

"None of this shit matters, Clay. None of it. First Joel, now Kenny. What does your ticket say? Why don't you show me your ticket?"

Clay blinks, tries to reach for her again, but she takes another step back.

"Harper, the edge," Clay says, watching the heel of her shoes come dangerously close to the embankment.

She looks at his hand hanging in the air between them. Tears spring to her eyes. "Oh my god," she says. "I can't believe I didn't see it before."

Clay shakes his head, confused. "See what?"

She points a finger at him. "You! You've been obsessed with me for months now. You think I don't see it? I do. You're the one who found the machine. You're the one who figured out what the fortunes say."

"What? No! I'm just trying to understand this."

She laughs without any humor. "Are you making this happen, Clay? Maybe that machine doesn't reveal a future that's already written. Maybe it tells *you* the future *you* wish would happen. What does your ticket say? Does it say you get the girl? Does it say...." She stops to swallow, eyes huge and wet and shimmering.

"No, I swear. I don't know how this all works, and I don't know if reading the fortune makes something happen, or if it only shows what was always going to happen."

She steps closer to him, hands clenched into fists and shaking. "What does your ticket say?"

"Harper, please stop."

Her voice lowers. "Tell me."

Clay can't look at her face anymore. "It says... it says I'll see what I don't want to see. And ever since Joel and I found that machine, it's been heartbreak after heartbreak. I don't want this! I'm just trying to figure out what we do next, if any of it can be fixed."

He glances back at her, and the words suddenly vanish. Clay shakes his head, looks away, and there's no fighting the tears that fall from his eyes. He believed that discovering the origin of the machine and the man who had built it might have provided some answers. Or at least a path forward. But Harper is right, none of it matters because it doesn't change anything.

Harper places one cold hand against Clay's chest and holds it there above his heart.

"They're just words on paper," she says. "They can't make things happen. That's not how the world works. Joel was going to test drive his car, whether you guys found the machine or not. And Kenny…." Her hand moves away from his chest, rises, and covers her face as she weeps.

Clay isn't sure what to do, how to fix anything, and he wonders if that's part of being an adult, too. Some things can't be fixed, and once they're broken, they'll always be that way.

As he holds his friend, Clay imagines he can feel the cracks forming in Harper as she sobs into his shoulder, as her ribs shake against his fingers. He imagines he's holding her together as she falls apart.

"I can't do this anymore, Clay," she sniffs and whispers. "Sometimes I feel like I'm barely making it, like I'm barely okay. And this is too much for me." She pulls away, slips one hand inside the sleeve of her sweatshirt, and wipes away the tears and makeup under her eyes.

"Last night, I lay in bed and I was hurting so bad I started thinking I'd do almost anything to make it stop. And for the first time in my life, I didn't want to be alive."

"No, no. Harper, please listen to me…"

Clay watches, terrified, as the girl he loves, one of his best friends in the world, transforms before his eyes into something he doesn't recognize. Her beauty collapses into sorrow. Her softness hardens into pain. Her eyes change shape from oval to circle, and back again. She is elegant and feral, thrumming with tense animal physicality as she opens and closes her hands.

"I couldn't think of any other way," she says. "I want to sleep and never wake up. I don't want to feel like this ever again. If this is what living is, then I don't want it. You know, I used to look at the future and see something worth running towards. But now, I realize the future is just more pain, more loss, again and again."

She smiles the saddest smile Clay has ever seen. "I don't want that. And all of this," waving a hand at the documents Clay had printed, "is just trying to make sense of something that is never going to make sense. Clay, I love you with all my heart, but I need to be away from you right now, and I need you to respect that. I don't want to hear these stories about mythical devices, and missing people, and all this darkness. Okay? It's all too dark. So, please, stay away from me. I'm not saying we can't still be friends, but for now I need you to stay away."

Clay tries not to let the words slice through his heart and slip into his bloodstream, but he can't stop them. He bites his lip to stop the tears, but they come anyway, and Harper smiles sadly and kisses his cheek with frozen lips.

She turns and walks down the bike path, away from him, until the mist swirls around her body and she's gone.

24

CLAY SITS ALONE LISTENING TO the river until he can no longer feel his hands. He wishes he could cry, just to have some release of all the hurt that he carries, but he doesn't have any more tears. In fact, he feels numb. First Joel, then his parents, then Kenny, and now Harper. Everything he loves is being torn away from him.

Maybe Harper's words weren't a prophecy so much as an examination of what's already happening. Maybe Clay is already living a nightmare.

He walks back to his car and feels a sudden sense of shame at how shitty and beat up it is. How could he ever think a girl would want to be picked up in something so cheap and ugly?

He has no idea where to go or what to do. Even the excitement he felt at figuring out where that Longsight machine came from is gone. What does it matter if he knows who built it?

Nothing changes.

Clay throws the stack of papers at the passenger seat. They burst and scatter.

He turns the key and drives out of the parking lot.

Fifteen minutes later, he's walking a hospital hallway to the ICU. He finds Joel alone in his room, the breathing tube still down his throat. Clay pulls a chair up close to the bed and touches his friend's arm. An IV is taped to the back of Joel's hand, pumping fluid into his vein.

The lacerations on his face have begun scab and heal. There will be scars. On the outside. More on the inside.

Clay thinks, *If this was a movie I'd talk to him. I'd tell him everything I learned, everything that's happened.*

But he doesn't even want to hear his own voice. Besides, he doesn't have the energy to speak. So he sits and squeezes Joel's hand, hoping the sensation travels through his comatose state, bypasses the drugs, and reaches his brain. Clay hopes Joel knows that he's there, by his side.

As he sits and listens to the breathing machine inhale and exhale, and the occasional beep from the monitor on the wall, Clay thinks about the Fright Fair, about how none of this will matter by tomorrow because tonight is the last night of the Fair.

"We never should have looked under that tarp," Clay whispers. "We never should have touched that machine."

25

CLAY AND HIS MOM EAT chicken and broccoli on the couch while watching a singing competition show on TV. Clay couldn't care less, but Mom used to love singing, and she enjoys watching all the talented performers on stage. She likes to act like she's one of the celebrity judges.

The house feels so different without Dad. At one point, during a commercial, Clay says, "When is—" and stops himself from finishing the thought, from asking when Dad is going to be home.

Mom looks over and says, "What?"

Clay shakes his head and says, "Nothing."

His phone buzzes from the cushion next to him. Clay picks it up and sees a text from Harper.

Please call me when you get this.

His heart aches a little, and he wonders if this is a test.

Girls, he thinks. *So confusing.*

He doesn't know what the right thing to do is. Dad once told him that sometimes girls will say one thing and mean another. Clay isn't sure that's exclusive to women, though, because he's pretty sure Dad does the same thing. In fact, he did it just the other night when he promised he'd see Clay just as often as he does now. How a transparent lie is supposed to make Clay feel better, he has no idea.

He sets the phone on "do not disturb" and turns his attention back to the TV.

They watch the show in silence. Mom, with her feet tucked underneath her, and a blanket draped over her lap. Clay looks at her in profile and feels a swell of gratitude that he has someone in his life as strong, selfless, and wise as his mother.

He wants to say it out loud. Why doesn't he? Why doesn't he say the things that appear in his head?

He reaches out and takes her hand, much the same way he held Joel's, and says, "I love you."

She smiles at him. "I love you, too, honey."

After Mom has gone to bed, Clay lies awake in his room, thinking about how he wants to text Kenny. The fact that his message would be sent to a melted puddle of plastic, glass, and microchips makes him break out in a cold sweat. He feels an emptiness in his life that has never been there before. An absence of things he always thought couldn't be lost.

He opens his phone and sees three missed texts. All of them from Harper.

I know you're hurt by what I said, but I really need to talk to you.

Please, please, please call me.

This can't wait. I'm really scared. Call me, please.

Clay could have easily ignored her texts, except that last one made his heart beat faster.

I'm really scared.

What if he called, and all she wanted was to rip him apart again? To say all the worst things she could think of?

Another lesson.

Sometimes, being an adult means letting yourself be hurt by someone you love. Sometimes, it means knowing the anger isn't directed at you. Not really.

Clay pushes the phone icon above Harper's name and holds the phone to his ear.

She picks up on the first ring.

26

HER VOICE IS SMALL AND frightened through the speaker. She sounds hoarse and congested.

Clay is determined to be bigger than his pain. He won't bring up what she said. He will act like it never even happened.

"Clay, oh my god! I'm so glad you called."

"Hey, what's up?" He tries to act normal, but his voice sounds flat, even to him.

She exhales loudly. "Listen, I'm so sorry about what I said. I don't really want you to stay away from me."

"It's okay."

"No, it's not. I'm hurt and I'm scared, and I took it out on you. That isn't right."

Clay closes his eyes. "I know. We'll talk about it later, okay?"

"Listen, things are not good at home right now. I know everything probably looks perfect from the outside, but it's not. It's pretty fucking far from perfect."

"I understand," Clay says.

"Do you?" Not accusatory. Hopeful.

Clay nods even though she can't see it. "I don't even think perfect really exists. Maybe only in movies."

"I'm sorry," Harper says quietly. "For all of it. I just feel… lost." There's a long pause. Her breathing has a hitch in it, like she's trying hard not to cry. "I went back, Clay. Oh my god, I went back."

"Back? Back where?"

More breathing. Panicked. "To the fair."

"Harper, no."

Her voice is quiet, the whisper of someone on the phone with the police while hiding from a killer. "I went back to the machine."

Clay's stomach drops. "No." The floor of his room plummets and becomes a chasm. His head spins, and the walls spin with it.

She swallows. "I was so depressed, so angry. And I just wanted to see the machine again. I don't know, see if maybe there was something we missed. Something that could fix this."

Clay's head feels detached from his body, floating somewhere near the ceiling like a balloon. "Tell me you didn't get a ticket. Please, Harper, tell me you didn't get one."

Silence.

Breathing.

Another swallow. A choked sob.

"Harper?"

Finally, she says, "I got a ticket."

Air rushes out of Clay's lungs. His hands are tingling with fire. "God damn it. Why would you do that?"

"I-I thought if something bad was going to happen to me, I wanted to know what it was."

Clay's scalp tightens over his skull and gives him a raging headache. He tries to keep his voice calm. "What does it say?"

More silence.

"Harper! What the fuck does it say?"

She sniffs and begins reading, and Clay can barely make out the words through her tears. His whole body suddenly feels feverish. A wave of dizziness and nausea overtakes him, and his stomach churns.

**UNDER MOON'S PALE LIGHT, A SHADOW CREEPS
A WALK TURNED DARK WHERE DANGER SLEEPS
A SCREAM UNHEARD, A FATE UNKIND
IN NIGHT'S EMBRACE, INNOCENCE DEFILED**

Where the other fortunes were vague and cryptic, there's a violence to Harper's. It feels less like a fortune and more like a threat. It can only be read one way—something horrific is going to happen to her, but there's no indication when it will occur. Could be tonight, could be a year from now.

Clay is buried so deep in his own thoughts that he doesn't hear Harper say, "What should we do?" the first time. She repeats herself, and Clay lies back on his bed because his body is too weak to sit up any longer. His pulse hammers against his temples.

"Don't leave the house," Clay says. "Not for anyone. Pretend to be sick, but don't let your parents take you to the doctor."

"Okay," Harper says in a small voice. Then, "Clay, do you really believe the machine knows what will happen, or is it just coincidence?"

To tell her he believed it would only add fuel to her fear, but to lie and say it was only a coincidence would downplay the severity of the situation.

Clay's eyes roam around his room, looking for answers. "We're going to fix this, okay? We'll figure out a way to keep you safe. I don't know how, but I'll think of something. You just have to stay home and be around people as much as possible. Hang out with your family. It seems like whatever happens will be when you're alone. I mean it, do not leave the house. Don't walk the dog, don't take out the trash. Don't even—"

"Clay?"

He didn't realize how fast he's been talking until she interrupted. His throat is raw, and he's out of breath.

"I'm sorry," Harper says. "I'm sorry about all of it."

She holds the phone away from her face and cries, and the sound is so broken, so vulnerable that Clay feels completely powerless. He wants to tell her everything will be fine, but he doesn't know that, and he can't promise it. He wishes he was with her, in her room, so he could hold her, comfort her.

He stares straight ahead at his bedroom wall, at the fist-sized hole he punched in it the other night. Heartache, violence, destruction.

"Harper, listen, I don't know if the machine predicts what is already going to happen, or if it makes these things happen… but I have an idea."

Her voice is thick with tears and snot. "Please don't go back to the machine. Please."

A dark jagged hole in a white wall, bleeding sheet-rock dust. He could have punched a thousand holes in that wall. He could have torn down the house. It burns inside him, all the hurt and anger. An inferno as white-hot and deadly as the one that burned down Kenny's house. He still feels it, simmering inside his chest.

"I'm going to go back to the Fair," Clay says gently, "and I'm going to destroy that fucking machine."

27

AFTER THEY HANG UP, CLAY swipes open his phone, and searches for the Fright Fair. Once he clicks on the website, a rotting ghost's face flies toward him on the screen and a woman's shrill scream blasts from the small speaker. Clay's whole body jerks, and he drops the phone onto the bed, heart thudding so fast his legs go weak.

He grabs the phone again, turns down the volume, taps the menu button, and selects "Schedule."

The Fair arrived in Medford on Thursday, November 7th. Each stop on the tour is four nights, which means November 10th is the last day before it leaves town. Clay swipes over to the calendar app and opens it.

His heart drops.

In the chaos of everything that's happened over the past few days, time seemed to unravel. Their first night at the Fair, Joel's accident, Kenny…all of it seems to exist simultaneously in the distant past and the burning now.

Clay's hand shakes as he looks at the date. November 10th.

Day four.

THE DUST OF TIME, IT SHIFTS AND SWAYS
THE CLOCK TICKS UNENDING, COUNTING DOWN FOUR DAYS

He looks at the clock. 11 p.m.

By tomorrow morning, the Fair will be disassembled, packed up, and taken to the next town, and the Longsight machine will be gone. Whatever he's going to do has to be done tonight.

28

THE HEADLIGHTS OF CLAY'S CAR punch holes in the dark as he speeds down backroads. The steering wheel is slick with sweat, the windshield foggy from his rapid breathing. He approaches a stop sign, slows down, then rolls through it and hits the gas. The old car groans as he pushes the speedometer past seventy miles per hour.

Before sneaking out of the house, Clay had gone into the garage and searched until he found the handheld metal shears Dad bought and used to trim pieces of gutter guard. The shears lie on the passenger seat along with a pair of leather work gloves.

The Fair has shut down for the night, and Clay knows this because the sky above the fairgrounds is dark.

No lights color the gray clouds.

Empty fields rush by. At another stop sign, Clay turns right and speeds past a recently built housing development. All brand new, two-story homes his family could never afford.

Soon, he drives over the interstate on a road that curves until it reaches the fairground.

The parking lot is empty. A few lights glow in the mist like ghosts hovering above the asphalt. Clay drives to the far end, where he and his friends had parked what seems like weeks ago.

Clay pulls into a slot far from the light, so his car is in shadow. He turns off the engine and waits. He should have eaten something before leaving the house, because now his blood sugar is dropping, making him feel weak and shaky.

He breathes in deeply and holds it until his lungs burn. Then, he forces himself to exhale slowly. His head feels hollow, light. He does it again.

Move with intention, he thinks. *Go straight for the machine and do not hesitate.*

Clay gets out of the car and stuffs the keys in his jacket pocket without locking the door. He doesn't want to fumble with unlocking the door if he needs to run, to make a fast getaway. He slips on the gloves and clenches his fists a few times to loosen up the leather. Then he grabs the shears and crosses the parking lot to the chain-link fence.

He stands at almost the exact same spot where they'd climbed a few days ago. Clay can still find all the emotions from that night. Just because nothing went as planned doesn't mean the feelings vanish. No, they were torn up like junk mail into tiny pieces of paper that drift and float through his subconscious. He remembers watching Harper climb the fence and the paralyzing shot of pure lust that raced through his body. He remembers the cold sting of her rejection, but he knows that's not fair to her. He never told her how he felt. He was too afraid. Maybe she felt rejected by him?

Another adult lesson, he thinks. Sometimes being an adult means understanding how everything you say, and everything you don't say, can cause pinball reactions. Instead of seeing himself as wronged by Harper and Kenny, he now sees his role in all of it, and with this realization comes a regret so sharp and heavy that his knees nearly buckle.

With one hand, he unlocks the shears and angles a link of fence between the blades. He squeezes the handles together and snips through the metal with a soft *tink*.

The storage tent lies just on the other side of the fence, flaps rustling in a gentle breeze. The rest of the fairgrounds are dark and quiet except for the occasional scratch of dead leaves that tumble across the walkways.

Clay listens, hears nothing, and resumes cutting open a hole in the fence big enough to climb through.

He snips through three sides of a small rectangle, then bends the section of fence like a door. Leaving the shears on the ground, Clay carefully moves his body through the space, avoiding the jagged metal edges. He moves quickly across the blacktop, keeping an eye out for the large bald man who'd chased them off the other night, or any other park employees. Staying low, in shadow, and creeps into the large storage tent.

The Longsight machine is unmistakable in the corner, covered once more by the canvas tarp. Clay approaches, one hand out, gloved fingers grazing the canvas, and grips a handful of tarp. His chest tingles like a limb that's fallen asleep, and tremors race down his arm, causing his hand to shake the canvas.

Clay pulls slowly and lets the tarp fall to the ground.

He doesn't want to look, but he does and jumps back when he sees the old man's dead eyes and creased face staring right back at him. Clay's heart feels drained of blood, an empty muscle pumping air through his arteries. He forces himself to stand up straight and stare right back at the lifeless man behind the glass. Clay wonders when Longsight had the likeness made. The animatronic. Or maybe he didn't commission it himself. Maybe whoever found and bought the machine had it constructed as a tribute to the man who built it.

When he and Joel first found the machine, Clay thought the expression on the man's face was angry, judgmental even. Like he found a perverse pleasure in revealing the horrible futures he saw. But now, as Clay leans in closer and inspects the lines that scatter from the old man's eyes, the deep grooves on either side of his mouth, the topographical map of his skin, he thinks the expression is one of sadness. There's anger too, but it looks more like the frustrated resignation of a prisoner rather than a madman.

Maybe that's all they are.

Longsight, Joel, Harper, Kenny, and Clay himself. Prisoners of the future, of an unseen world pressing against them, crushing them under its weight a little more each day.

Clay no longer thinks of the old man as a creepy animatronic, but as a tragic statue.

He turns in a circle, searching for the mallet he'd seen the last time he was here. A mallet with a broken handle, used in the "Frankenstein's Test of Strength" game. He moves aside some of the cardboard boxes, pushing them out of the way until he sees the mallet leaning against a metal shelving unit.

Clay picks it up and it's heavier than he thought it would be—the hammer end is solid rubber.

Based on the two photographs from Longsight's garage workshop, there should be a panel on the lower right side of the machine. Gripping the mallet in both hands, Clay eyes the machine, already aiming in his head, and wonders what he expects.

Images pop in his mind like camera flashes. Quick and violent pictures of Harper being attacked from behind, strong hands gripping her shoulders and shoving her to the ground. Clay blinks and shakes his head, but the images keep coming, one after the other. A face leaning so close to hers that she can smell his foul breath. She fights, God, how she fights him as his fingers struggle for the button of her jeans, yanking, pulling, until the skin of her bare legs feels the cold grit of sidewalk concrete. She spits in his face, gnashes her teeth when his lips get too close. Using her nails like claws, she scratches the man's face deep enough to draw blood. Enraged, he grabs a fistful of her hair and slams her head down, cracking her skull. Warm blood leaks, black as oil in the moonlight. They've fallen near some trash cans and knocked over a recycling container. Glass beer and liquor bottles clink and roll out. One of them breaks under the attacker's boots. His hand blindly reaches until he finds a green chunk of glass that glitters, and he holds it like a knife, the edges so sharp that Harper doesn't even feel the dozens of slices until her skin splits open and cold air caresses the wounds.

Clay tries to shut his eyes against the horror, but his eyes are already closed. He sees his fear projected in his mind. Harper's ticket comes to vivid life, and his stomach clenches as he hears her scream for help that never comes.

TRAPPED INSIDE YOUR MIND'S OWN JAIL
WHAT YOU DO NOT WISH TO SEE WILL BE UNVEILED

What does he expect?

Inside that machine, a device older than the oldest thing he's ever seen. A disk that somehow communicates from a day, an hour, a time that does not yet exist, and transmits a vision from this place to the user. If Clay can hold that in his hands, maybe he can see another version of the future, a place in which Harper is okay, and Joel wakes up. Maybe Mom and Dad are together in this place, and everything that doesn't make sense has an answer. Maybe the Earth spins backwards and remakes everything that's been lost.

"I've seen enough," Clay whispers. "I don't want to see anymore."

Clenching his jaw and suppressing a yell, Clay pulls back the hammer and swings at the machine with all his strength. A hollow echo resounds within the box, wood splinters, and Clay swings again and again, like each dull crack can reset the past and remake the future. Sweat and tears stinging his eyes, Clay swings one last time, and the mallet smashes through to the other side.

29

STALE AIR POURS OUT OF the hole in the wood, the odor of old things that have decayed and turned to dust. Clay covers his nose and mouth with an arm and waves the cloud of dust away from his face. He peers into the darkness of the machine. A quiet click echoes inside, so subtle he wonders if it's a mouse nibbling on something. Tiny teeth gnawing.

Clay drops the mallet and looks over his shoulder to see if the noise has drawn any attention. The fairgrounds remain silent and empty. He digs his phone from his pocket and turns on the flashlight, angling it so it doesn't light up the whole tent, then he kneels and crawls forward until his face is right next to the hole.

He points the flashlight and peers inside.

A thick layer of dust coats the bottom, deep enough to scrawl his name in. Two broad support beams covered in brown fabric connect to the panel that separates the machinery from the animatronic.

He crawls forward a little further, sticking his head through the opening and shining the light deeper into the box. He squints. He expected to see a tangle of wires, hydraulics, and cables all connected to a motor, but the box is almost entirely empty except for the supports and something round on the floor between them, buried beneath inches of dust.

Holding the phone in one hand, he leans forward, putting all his weight on his elbow, and reaches out with the other hand to brush dust off the circular object. His mouth has gone dry, and dust particles are pulled into his sinuses with each breath. His heartbeat seems so loud, louder even than the hammering. It pulses in his ears, pushes so hard against his eyes that it hurts to blink.

His fingers wipe dirt from the object, revealing cold, gray stone with enigmatic symbols carved into its surface. Symbols that look like a language he's never seen in any history book. Straight lines of varying lengths and sizes, some of which curve into half circles and spheres.

He holds his breath, and there is silence.

"This is it," he whispers. "I was right."

His arm brushes one of the supports, and the brown fabric moves. He feels something within it, something thin and round. A rod of some kind.

Placing his hand flat on the surface of the object, he wipes more dust until he sees the fullness of the disk, as big and round as a dinner plate with an opening at the center. He realizes now that the device is actually two disks connected by a metal ring with grooves. The second disk contains a different set of symbols.

He slides his fingers under the disk to lift it up. The clicking he heard gets louder. He points the flashlight around the box, searching for the rodent making the sound.

Click, click, click

Loud. The scrape of metal against stone.

Clay swings the light back to the disk. It's moving, the inner circle grinding against the outer, bringing certain symbols into alignment. The clicking stops, and there's a deep, yet quiet hum. The skin on the back of Clay's neck feels electrified as a blue light appears at the center of the disk. At first, it looks like smoke trapped beneath water. A swirling constellation of pinpoint lights caught in turquoise currents.

Light fills the box, and Clay turns his head away, lowering his other hand to the floor to back out. His hand touches something cold and slick at the base of the support, his fingers feel the shape of it, and in the blue light, he realizes what it is. A leather shoe.

The smoke and liquid continue swirling in the disk, growing brighter and more intense.

Clay gently touches the support beam again and nearly screams when his fingers curl around it.

It's not a support beam at all. It's a leg. Two legs draped in brown pants.

"Holy shit," Clay whispers. "It's him."

He understands. It's not just a torso in the upper half of the box. A complete man stands inside the machine.

He never disappeared. Clay's memory flashes back to Longsight's notes on his experiments. He brought drums full of sacred water back with him from Greece. Water that the Oracles used to protect their minds from the powerful visions.

Longsight wrote that he ran out of water just as the visions were becoming clear and sustained. Overwhelmed with an onslaught of images of events that had yet to occur, the man became frozen in place. A conduit for whatever the transmissions from the future the disk received.

Clay plants both hands against the floor and pushes backward just as there is a final click so loud it rattles his teeth. The light in the disk turns bright white, so blinding that Clay has to shut his eyes.

He feels the cool air outside the box blow across his neck as he backs out. He ducks his head to avoid cutting it on the splintered wood. The disk is vibrating now, rattling on the wooden floor. A steadily increasing mechanical hum like a hive of angry bees.

He opens his eyes just as a gnarled hand shoots down from the upper half of the box. Skeletal fingers wrap around his wrist so tightly his bones grind together. The hand pulls him, smashing his face against the side of the box. His nose snaps, and blood pours down into his mouth.

Clay screams, "No! Help! Help me, please!"

The hand jerks harder. Clay's neck wrenches with a sickening crack. Dust spills from the hole in the center panel like sifted ash. With his cheek mashed against the wood, he twists just enough to look up—only to meet the glowing stare of Henry Longsight. The man's face leers through the glass, teeth set in a wicked grin. Cracks spiderweb across his skin, splitting it in jagged, unnatural lines. His jaw unhinges. His eyes roll back. Then, slowly, horribly, his face begins to collapse inward—flaking into dust, layer by layer, flowing off the skull in waves. The powder drifts down, thick as smoke, settling over Clay's arm like ash.

With a final wrench that cracks Clay's eye socket against the wood, the bony hand drags the teenager into the box. Clay's screams of pain, his screams for help, are choked out as Longsight's body collapses into a thick cloud of dust that rains down and fills Clay's open mouth, snuffing out his voice and then, consciousness.

SOUTHBOUND ON I-5

WHEN THE SUN RISES, THE employees of Fright Fair exit their trailers, yawning and stretching. They stumble to the mess tent where the cook has set out metal pans of scrambled eggs and sausage. A crew of men and women eat, drink coffee, and slowly wake up before beginning the painstaking process of breaking down and loading all the decorations, costumes, equipment, games, and prizes back onto the trucks.

Hours pass under gray skies that threaten to storm at any minute. A chill and an electricity course through the air.

A large bald man with tattoos on his neck, wearing blue coveralls, and smoking a cigarette, shuffles to the storage tent. This tent is always the first to be unloaded, and the last to be loaded when they leave. Sometimes, Harvey wonders why they bother to haul this junk around at all.

He stops when he enters the tent and stares at the fortune-telling machine in the corner. The tarp has come off again, and pieces of broken wood lie on the ground next to a hole in its side.

Harvey has never liked the machine. In fact, he hates how much the old man resembles his father. Enough to make Harvey's muscles tense at the sight of the fortune teller's wrinkled face.

He approaches, then stops and stares, his mouth falling open. The cigarette falls from between his fingers and hits the concrete in a small shower of orange sparks.

The old man is gone, and in his place is a kid. A teenager who stares back with a cold and vacant expression, eyes wide and glassy. The skin between those colorless eyes is slightly folded, giving the kid an intensity that's unnerving.

The old man was bad, but this kid might even be worse. He looks acidic, almost cruel.

Harvey taps the side of his head twice with the heel of one hand. Ever since his boxing days, the world sometimes skips forward and backward, and he's not always certain of things that should be certain.

Was there ever an old man in that machine, or was he just seeing a projection? Did he see his father because of all that hate he still carries in his heart? Was it always a teenager? And why does this kid look familiar?

Harvey lets out a little growl because he doesn't like it when things don't make sense. He certainly isn't going to say anything and risk sounding crazy. His boss would probably fire him on the spot if he were wrong.

So, Harvey decides to keep his head down and complete the task.

His knees are bad, so he reaches out and grabs the metal lever on the machine to steady himself as he kneels to pick up all the broken wood and tosses it into the hole. With his hand on the lever, something inside the machine begins to hum. Harvey stands quickly and backs away. The teenager's eyes are glowing, and the curled fingers of one hand wave back and forth over a crystal ball that ignites with blue light.

There is a brief mechanical whir, and a second later, a ticket appears in the slot.

The convoy is on the road. A caravan of semi-trucks and buses, traveling south on the interstate to the next town on their schedule.

Harvey sits on one of the buses, staring out the window as the landscape rushes past in a blur of green trees, gray skies, and clouds burning purple and red.

Many of the other employees drink and play cards on the drive. Laughing, smoking, telling stories. The noise usually bothers him, but today he is distracted, troubled even.

For years, Harvey thought that if something bad was going to happen to him, it would be on this highway. This endless stretch of blacktop cuts through mountains, forests, lakes, and rivers. It would be this interstate, with all its secrets and mysteries, its bloodstained asphalt and scarred dividers, that would be his end.

And now, he holds in his sweaty hand a ticket that seems to confirm all his worst fears.

As the vehicle races down the highway, chasing sunlight to another nowhere town, he cannot stop thinking about what the ticket says.

THANKS

To Steve Berman, Ben Baldwin, Scott Cole, Elizabeth Copps, Alec Frankel.

To Mitch Hull, Brennan LaFaro, Phil Haagensen, Jason Horneck, and Brad England for early reads and feedback.

To the incredible folks who support me on Patreon, I'm so grateful for each of you.

To the Statue Tier Patrons:

Mike Hughes, Shaun Rosel, Paul Miller, Brandon Sharp, Kevin Heimann, John Fahey, David Swisher, Steven

Duane Allison Junior, Phil Haagensen, Rob Dolan, Jason Murphy, Jason Horneck, Joshua Perez, Roberto Hull, Thomas Clink, Thomas Finnegan, Brandon Carr, Brad England, Zachery Long, Erik Mann, David Perry, and Alexia Simms.

You are all golden.

As always, to Rae Lyn, Liam, and Quinn. Thank you for a beautiful future.